THE NIGHTMARE COLLECTION

VOLUME 1

LEE MOUNTFORD

THE HOBBES HALL DIARIES

1-1

Preface
by Dr. Addington

I 'acquired' this diary only three weeks ago. At first, I was skeptical about it, thinking it nothing more than fiction. However, I have since looked into the matter further and made my own inquiries. I am now of the opinion that the events outlined in the following diary are somehow linked to my ongoing investigations.

Whilst Hobbes Hall itself seems to be the narrator's main focus, I think the other plane (a term I use in absence of any other) had somehow seeped into the abandoned asylum. It is this 'other plane,' and the nightmarish descriptions given about it, that interest me most. And this is the reason for its inclusion in my records.

The original digital file—from a word processor file—is transferred here as I originally found it, with no alterations.

- Dr. Phillip Addington, 2019.

1-2

8th August 2014 - Part 1

My name is Andrew Clementine. I am twenty-seven years old and am of sound mind.

Or at least, I thought I was. Regardless, I'm terrified that I will die soon.

I've never been one for keeping a diary, never really thought it would be my kind of thing—probably isn't—but I guess *needs must as the devil drives*, as they say.

I'm not looking to note down everyday life events or express my inner feelings. There is a genuine need for this. I want this document to be a record of what I've found. Of that place.

And what has been happening to me.

Writing it all down may help me make sense of everything, but—if I'm being honest with myself—I know I am really doing this because I'm scared.

Scared of what is happening. And of what will happen.

It may sound paranoid, but I don't think I will survive what is happening. So it brings me small comfort to know that, if the worst should happen, then someone could read my account and know the truth.

Or as much of the truth as is possible to know.

Nothing that has happened so far is evidence that my life is being threatened directly, but events have been... strange. It may be a bit of a leap for some people to think that I am in any real danger.

And maybe that is true.

I hope it is.

But I don't *believe* that it is.

So, in order for this diary to make sense to you, whoever you are, I need to bring you up to speed.

I've thought long and hard about every detail and tried to ensure that dates and descriptions given are as accurate as possible. If any errors are present, then I apologise, and can only assure you that I have been as truthful and honest as my memory would allow.

The following pages—which will give a brief history of what has happened to me thus far—will be presented in italics for clarity.

1-3

17th March 2013

I include this date and passage not because it has anything to do with what has been going on as of late, but so that you can understand who I am and what I do.

Or did.

For two years prior to my accident I and four others partook in a pastime known as 'urban exploration.' The other four in my group were Keith Hemway, Phil Jacobs, Aaron Tyler, and Anthony Pearson. Keith and I grew up together, and we met the others at university. We all became close friends, keeping in touch long after we left higher education, and met up as often as we could.

It was Phil who introduced us all to urban exploring—the pastime of looking around abandoned buildings and deserted areas of interest. Most of the time we weren't supposed to be in any of the places we visited, but that added to the thrill and appealed to our adventurous natures.

I will admit that it was always a fantastic rush to see these abandoned buildings, to think about their histories, and to find something that human eyes had not seen in a long time. And you would be surprised to learn just how many forgotten places there are in a country as populated as ours.

On the 17th of March—I remember this date well—we all headed to the Midlands to explore an abandoned school. Anthony, a local to the area, made the find. It was a good one too—the place was huge.

At dusk, we broke in (there is no other term for it—that's exactly what we did) and started on our mini-adventure. And it was around nine-thirty when it happened. Aaron and I were ascending an old flight of stairs when the treads gave way.

Aaron managed to hold on.

I fell through onto a banister below and broke my back.

Three days later, in a hospital bed, I was told I would never walk again. So far, that prognosis has proved to be entirely accurate.

I was depressed for months after losing the ability to walk, and it took me a long time to find any kind of hope. But, eventually, I resolved to move on with my life and make the best of it.

It was hard, but I tried to limit the extent to which my disability held me back. And for a time, I actually felt like I was making progress toward being happy again.

Then my girlfriend of four years, Stacy Peterson, broke down and told me it was just too much for her. She ended things with me, breaking my heart.

I haven't seen or heard from her since.

Again, I'll be honest that this affected me more than I was able to admit at the time. Also, my friends had started exploring again, something I was now incapable of taking part in, and I began to see less and less of them.

All promises that 'we'll be here for you no matter what' proved to be hollow. I guess it's easy to say it in the moment, but much more difficult to follow through on. As much as it hurt, I *guess I can understand Stacy's decision. It was a selfish one, but she was young and had her own life to live.*

However, the attitude of my so-called friends, I will say, fucking pissed me off.

Still does.

I may not have been able to do anything adventurous, but I refuse to believe that spending time with me was so difficult. As it was, the times I did see them grew fewer and fewer, until they dried up completely.

With nothing else to keep me in my home town—only memories I wanted to forget—I eventually relocated further north.

1-4

15th July 2014

In early April I moved to County Durham in the North East of England. And I remember that on this particular day I was feeling pretty down. I'd found out that Stacy had got together with Keith. On top of that, I was struggling financially, which was one of the reasons I'd chosen this area to move to. (The other being my family roots here.) The compensation for my injury was meagre—I'd broken into an abandoned building and was owed, I found out, very little. So I found that money, or the lack of it, was a constant issue and strain—even with disability benefits.

My new house was small (a terraced property) and even though it felt a little like a fresh start, it was a lonely place.

So I took to going out as often as I could.

Life in a wheelchair is difficult. It is not until you are in one of these chairs permanently that you come to find it is restrictive in ways able-bodied people can never really comprehend.

There was nothing in the immediate vicinity that really held my interest, so I took to using what little money I had to ride the local bus routes and see a bit more. It didn't take me long to get to know the area.

On the 15th July 2014, I travelled to a nearby town.

About twenty minutes into the journey along a winding country road, I noticed a building ahead. It was predominantly red brick and looked run down and tired—clearly abandoned. Its windows were boarded with black plywood, which had white ribs painted on to imitate window frames.

The building was vast. Not a house, far too big for that. More like an old facility of some kind.

Its design seemed authoritarian, if that makes sense. Nothing really fancy or spectacular; rather, it was all business. Functional. Not in the least concerned with aesthetic value. I spied its over-grown drive coming to meet the very road we were on. Drawn to it, and with nothing better to do, I disembarked the bus at the next stop—annoyingly half a mile down the road. It took almost everything I had in my arms to wheel my chair down the cobbled, cracked footpath back to the driveway entrance.

I remember reaching the end of the long, worn tarmac entrance road, and I stared at the daunting structure. It had an imposing quality, and, though I have no idea why, I felt a pull. Something drew me to that place. I headed through the tall brick pillars at the entrance and down towards the building itself.

Was I looking for a way in? Even now, I'm not sure what was driving me at the time.

Every door that I could see was securely fastened with the same black-painted boarding I'd seen from the road. Although there were no houses around, I didn't want to try to rive one of these boards free on the off chance a passing car saw me from the road behind. I think I was contemplating heading around to the back when I heard it.

Muffled voices from within.

I couldn't tell from where they originated exactly—from

which window the sound came—but I heard them all the same. I listened more intently. Although I couldn't make out what was being said, I could definitely hear two distinct voices.

And that's when the banging and screaming started.

The boards on the windows shook, all of them, as if hundreds of people were banging from the rooms within, and these crashes were accompanied with screams of pain—hundreds of tortured voices unleashing their anguish.

There were countless windows along the front of the building, and from behind each one came desperate shrieks and loud, crashing sounds. The noises grew louder and louder, like a crescendo, and panic gripped my body.

I'd never felt like that before. Ever. Fear so immediate that I could barely move.

I remember my breathing becoming frantic, and I managed to put my hands to my ears to block out the fearful sounds. I wanted to run, I wanted to be able to use my legs again to get away from this place, but I was frozen in terror.

I don't know how long I waited—eyes closed, hands over my ears—before I realised that all was quiet.

Not a sound.

Was it all in my head?

I didn't hang around to find out. Adrenaline kicked in, and I wheeled my chair harder than ever. I don't remember much as I fled, and my first real memory was being back at the bus stop, panting and feeling nauseous. I remember leaning over the side of my chair and vomiting until nothing was left in my belly.

Then things went black.

My next memory is of waking up, on the ground, next to the bus stop. A concerned passerby had stopped to help me. He quizzed me about what had happened. I just lied and told him I'd simply felt ill.

He offered to take me home, and I readily accepted. The kind stranger even helped me into the car and stowed my chair in the boot.

When I regained some form of composure, I asked if he knew about the abandoned building close to where he found me. He didn't know much, just that it was an old sanatorium, but he couldn't remember its name.

That night, part of me wanted to find out more about the place, and I was tempted to look online. But another part of me was still terrified at what I'd witnessed. I remember being uneasy that night. Just being alone in the house as darkness set in was enough to unnerve me. I felt like someone was there with me, creeping around in the shadows. Watching me. And I was constantly on edge.

So, in the end, I resolved not to investigate the building any farther.

But that didn't last.

1-5

25th July 2014

In the days that followed I went against my initial resistance—and my better judgement—and looked up the abandoned building, aiming to find out anything I could about it. I don't know why (this is a common theme, I fear), but I just could not get that place out of my head.

But my search turned up very little. I used to think that Google and the internet were all-knowing, but I quickly found out there are certain subjects about which even the internet only knows tidbits at best.

What I did find, however, was the name of the building.

Hobbes Hall.

The only other information I dug up told me that the hall had indeed been a tuberculosis sanatorium, as well as a mental asylum for a time (or 'lunatic asylum,' as the search brought up —not a very PC term, but that was how it was known back then). The building was founded in 1925 and abandoned in 1997.

This wasn't out of the ordinary, it seemed. Whilst searching, I turned up dozens of other abandoned asylums in the North East alone, all with varying amounts of information, and not many lasted longer than this one. But I could not find out anything else about Hobbes Hall. Every link that promised more info turned out to be dead.

But that was not enough for me. The thought of the large, foreboding building ate away at me. It was always at the back of my mind, vying for attention.

And so, I made a grave mistake.

On 25th July 2014, I went back to Hobbes Hall.

I wanted to know for sure if what I had witnessed was real, or if it had been only in my head. The idea that it had all just been in my head was a scary thought, and the only way I could think to reconcile it was to go back and find out for certain.

I took the same bus route and wheeled myself again along the half mile from the bus stop to the entrance. The brick pillars either side of the drive flanked me as I looked down to Hobbes Hall. The sight of it caused by breath to catch in my throat.

I was scared, but moved onwards and down the driveway, towards the large building. It looked even more imposing this time, yet still I pressed on. Looking back now, I can't be certain if I was in complete control of what I was doing. And when I reached the building, I waited, despite my fear.

I had to know.

But there were no screams, no shrieks, no voices. No banging and crashing. Nothing out of the ordinary. I actually remember the chirping of birds.

Everything was normal.

I waited as long as I dared, and would have stayed longer but for a headache, probably born out of stress, that developed. Strong and intense. But as for the hall and the noises—nothing happened.

A huge sense of relief washed over me, and I turned and left. Almost entirely without incident.

Almost.

As I travelled back up the long driveway to the main road ahead, a sudden feeling gripped me, like I was being watched. I turned around and, upon inspection, noticed a window on the second floor was now without its boarding. I could see through the dirty glass, and I swear someone was there, standing motionless and looking out.

At me.

I squinted in the sun. Was I seeing someone, or was it just shadow, or maybe a curtain?

The longer I looked, the more I was sure that, in fact, no one was there. A trick of the brain, perhaps?

So I left and got the bus back to town, hoping I could now let this odd, unexplainable obsession go.

And I wish I could have.

But, when I returned home, there was a letter waiting for me on my entrance mat. The envelope was faded yellow and completely blank. I opened it and pulled out a single page—a note that contained the following message:

I SAW YOU AT MY HOME. YOU HEARD THE CRIES OF THE BLESSED. I AM WATCHING YOU NOW. AND THEY ARE WATCHING YOU, TOO.

1-6

4th August 2014

On the 3rd of August, 2014, I received another letter. This one simply stated: COME VISIT US AGAIN SOON.

I also received a few telephone calls on my landline, which were nothing but static (although in one, I swear I could hear something through the static—someone crying in pain).

I had not been back to Hobbes Hall at this point, and did not intend to go. But I was scared.

Terrified.

The letters that arrived had no distinguishing marks on them, and I had no idea who had sent them.

Was it someone playing a joke?

On top of that, I had been having terrible dreams, almost every night. Dreams that left me with a sense of palpable dread, but the content of them were, sadly, ambiguous to me after waking.

I remember thinking long and hard about what to do. Go to the police? Call someone for help?

Neither option seemed a good one. What could the police do? No crime had been committed. And who could I call for help? So, I came up with an unorthodox plan. But I had decided I would not just sit back and wait for whoever sent these letters to torment me further.

I would act.

And so, I went online and found a community of explorers who were somewhat close to the area and began to use my knowledge of the pastime to integrate myself with them.

Over the span of a few days, I posted constantly on the message-board, hoping to speed things up, and opened up about my past and my accident in the hope it would draw some sympathy.

And it worked.

I seemed to get on well with their online personalities, and I soon brought up Hobbes Hall, saying I'd seen it only in passing, but that it looked interesting. A place that someone should check out.

I wasn't proud of myself for my subterfuge, but that didn't stop me. I wasn't doing this to make new friends—although I could do with some replacements in all honesty—but because I wanted further knowledge of what Hobbes Hall was. After all, knowledge could be power, but I was ashamed that I wasn't prepared to go and get this knowledge for myself.

Regardless, I swallowed my shame and pressed on.

A few members of the group had heard of the place, but they didn't know too much about it, and none had gotten around to exploring it (though it was on some of their to-do lists).

My suggestion, thankfully, seemed raise their interest, and Hobbes Hall proved a great draw to them. A few of them arranged to make a trip on the 4th of August, around midnight, and spend a few hours there. I'd asked one of the members, Chris

—online persona Croona12—to fill me in on the details after the expedition, which he promised to do, saying he would get back to me the following day.

1-7

5th August 2014

I received no word back from anyone regarding the trip—despite my emails and posts on the message boards on this day.

1-8

6th August 2014

On the 6th, I received an email back from Chris.

It was brief:

NOT SURE WHAT HAPPENED THERE, MAN, AND DON'T REALLY WANT TO TALK ABOUT IT, TO BE HONEST. EVERYONE IS FREAKED OUT. I'M NOT SURE IF WE'LL BE KEEPING THIS SHIT UP ANYMORE. DO YOU KNOW ANYTHING ABOUT THIS PLACE? WAS THERE A REASON YOU SUGGESTED IT? DID YOU KNOW WHAT WOULD HAPPEN???

I emailed him back, just saying that I'd only seen the place but knew nothing about it. But I also added that if he wanted to talk about it, then I'd listen.

I made sure he knew I wasn't going to judge, no matter what he said to me. In his eventual response, he seemed grateful for that, and it sounded like he did actually want to talk to someone. Why he couldn't talk to the others, I had no idea, but it seemed like he had nowhere else to turn. No one was willing to listen.

I knew how that felt.

We arranged to meet up to discuss things in a local pub on the night of the 8th. It was a touch weird, knowing I was going to meet someone in person I'd only spoken to via email. And it was also a person I was lying to. All so that I could further my own growing obsession.

I didn't feel good about that. But, again, it didn't stop me.

1-9

7th August 2014

Another phone call on this day.

   More static.

   But this time I could clearly hear something within the electric crackling.

   Giggling.

   Maniac giggling.

1-10

8th August 2014 - Part 2

And that's pretty much all there is to know, so far. Those are the events that have scared me so and led me to this point.

They may be nothing, may be something, but they are significant enough that I will keep this diary going forward, for as long as I need to (or as long as I am able to).

I don't sleep much now, but the dreams—or nightmares —that consume me when I do seem very real.

Even after I wake, it takes me a few moments to figure out what was a dream and what is reality.

And the places in my dreams... such horrible places. Sometimes I am in Hobbes Hall (or what I assume to be Hobbes Hall, having never been inside), but other times I am somewhere else completely.

Somewhere indescribable.

Not of this world. Not of this reality. A nightmarish hellscape of madness and malevolence.

But back to reality. Back to the here and now. It is

roughly 5.45pm as I write this, and I'll soon be leaving to meet with Chris. I'm not sure what he's going to tell me, but I have a feeling I won't like it.

And yet, for a reason I can't explain (there it is again), I want more than anything to know.

1-11

9th August 2014

I met with Chris last night, as planned, and after an initial uncomfortable greeting, he finally went into detail about what happened on the 4th. I could tell it wasn't easy for him to relay, and he struggled with much of his story. As he spoke, I think he was gauging my reaction to see if I believed what he was saying or not. But every time he stalled, I urged him to go on.

And this is his tale, as closely as I can remember:

Chris and his group (Kirsty and Steve) met at Chris' house at roughly 11.00pm, before taking his car to the location (which they found relatively easily thanks to my directions). They drove down the driveway to the building and parked behind an overgrown hedge to obscure the car from view to anyone passing by on the road.

With their standard equipment—flashlights, cameras (both photograph and video), safety boots, dust masks, and harnesses—they explored the perimeter first. From Chris' description, it was just as I'd seen—lots of boarded up windows, with no obvious point of access. So, they gained entry by forcing free one of the window-boards and breaking the glass pane behind.

Upon getting inside, the group seemed to be in a small, ground-floor office, containing a desk, which was cluttered with papers and dust, and locked cabinets. Chris told me he had flicked through some of the papers on the desk and found that they were patient reports, but the handwriting was too difficult to read or really make sense of. They began photographing and recording as they moved from the office and out into the hallway.

Abandoned, desolate, intriguing, but not entirely remarkable—that was how Chris described the place to me. Yet as he spoke, his eyes warned that what was to come would prove that statement incorrect.

They searched the various rooms and corridors, excited by a new location to explore. Steve, however, had become restless, and hinted that they'd seen enough and should leave, which was apparently unlike him. When asked why, he wouldn't elaborate.

Something had spooked him.

The other two ignored him and continued to the first floor, with Steve reluctantly following. When upstairs, they found many rooms that seemed to be set up for patients in care. Old beds were still in some of these rooms, as well as empty drips, discarded needles, and other instruments that seasoned explorers knew to be wary of. It was while they were in one of these rooms that they heard it—a shriek coming from somewhere in the hallway.

From Chris' description, the group was understandably startled by what they'd heard, and he told me of the fear and confusion on his friends' faces.

Figuring the place wasn't as empty as they had first

thought, the three of them discussed the possibility of someone else being in the building. Maybe someone who was trapped, or hurt.

Chris yelled back, hoping for a response, but was met with nothing but silence.

At first.

Then the screaming began again—constant shrieks of pain of enormous intensity, as if someone were being butchered alive.

Steve demanded they leave but was overruled by the others who felt they should help whoever it was that was yelling. They were scared, of course, but their overriding thought was that someone was in distress and needed assistance.

Admirable.

They ran from the room and headed towards the source of the noise, shouting back as they ran, asking the stranger if he or she was hurt.

They followed the shrieks down the corridor to a room at the far end, its double doors closed. Chris, leading the way, frantically pushed and pulled at the doors, but found them locked.

He told of how the screaming increased in intensity, and they began kicking and ramming the door. Eventually, the aged, worn lock gave way, and the group spilled into the room, only to be greeted by an instant, dead silence.

No one was inside.

The cries of pain that had thundered around them stopped the very moment they gained entry. There was no one present.

The room itself was just like many others they'd seen, except the beds here were heavily stained with a dry, dark substance.

Steve insisted it was blood and again reiterated the need to flee.

It seemed this latest development swung everyone round to Steve's way of thinking, and they sprinted back the way they'd come.

As Chris ran, he turned to look back towards the room where the screaming had originated. He didn't know why he felt the need to look—perhaps out of fear and instinct—but in doing so he saw something I don't think he wanted to remember.

A lone figure was standing motionless in the corridor behind them, watching them as they ran. This person was heavily bandaged around the face, the faded white material stained orange and red. He, if it was indeed a *he*, made no attempt to move or follow.

Chris screamed to the others, ordering them to—in his words—*fucking run*.

They navigated back to their entry point, and Chris told me of how he muscled himself to the front and threw himself through the window they'd broken earlier, cutting his arm on a jagged piece of glass in the process. The others climbed out after him. As they ran back to the car, Kirsty demanded to know what he had seen.

Chris was apparently unable to answer at first, close to tears. Just seeing that person in the hallway, somehow so close to them, had filled him with a profound fear. After a moment of silence between us, Chris admitted to me that he thought that strange person was somehow... unnatural.

He went on.

Only when they were clear of the drive, and a mile down the road, was Chris calm enough to tell the others what he thought he had seen. He assumed they would call him crazy, but instead they said nothing. The group didn't speak much for the rest of the drive back.

In fact, Chris then told me that he hadn't spoken to the others at all since that night. And he showed me the wound on his arm, wrapped in a crude, self-applied bandage.

He was clearly struggling with what had happened. I had no idea what to say to his story, other than to tell him I believed it. Every word.

I think he appreciated that.

Again, I felt guilty for putting them in this situation in the first place. I had known something was very wrong with that place, yet I still sent them there to find out more, for my own ends.

And guilt wasn't the only emotion troubling me. A huge sense of dread washed over me, and it has not left since.

Everything Chris told me, I believe to be true. There is something dreadfully wrong with that place, something I do not understand, and something profoundly sinister. I have a feeling of foreboding—of uncertainty—at what may lie ahead, and I cannot shake it.

I just know something bad is going to happen.

And that is everything I have to say about my meeting with Chris. I'm tired as I write this, so I'm going to turn in for the night. I doubt I'll get much sleep, as I know the kind of dreams that will be waiting for me.

It's as if that place calls out to me though my subconscious.

And worse, some part of me seems to want to heed that call.

1-12

Today I decided that I didn't want to sit around the house all day. I felt that if I stayed inside, I'd only be able to think about one thing, and that would drive me crazy. So I went into town, I looked around, and I kept moving, hoping to keep my mind active. Distracted.

Some of the time it worked, but most of the time it didn't.

I returned home later that evening to find another letter waiting for me, in the same type of faded envelope, with another typed note inside.

Its message was no less ambiguous and disturbing: MISSING YOU, ANDREW.

This was my third note in all, but it is the first to refer to me by name.

These letters have obviously been hand delivered, as there is no stamp or address on the envelope. Which means someone has been calling to my house to deliver them.

The whole thing is getting to me. I no longer feel safe in my own home.

Also, Chris emailed me with an attachment—one of the photographs he'd taken during his visit to Hobbes Hall. He'd finally plucked up the courage to look through his digital files, and this one in particular showed something disturbing.

The photo was of a large room, lined with empty beds. At first glance there wasn't much to see, but when I looked closer, I could make out a distinct figure at the far end of the room, standing against the wall.

It was little more than a shadow, but undeniable in its shape and appearance.

The thing is, the camera is pointing directly towards it. There is no way the photographer could have missed it.

Yet Chris is adamant that when he took the picture, he saw nothing.

I sometimes wonder if returning to that place one final time may resolve things for me, one way or another. I know logically that it is not a wise idea, but still, I feel drawn to that place.

Another restless night awaits, I fear.

1-13

News!

I'm not sure if it's good or bad exactly, but for some reason it makes me feel better.

It all came about through a simple conversation with a neighbour, Ms. Goddard—an elderly lady who lives across the street. We don't speak often, but when we do bump into each other, I make a point of being pleasant and friendly—I think because she is alone and doesn't really have anyone.

Something I understand all too well.

I was on my way back from the local store with a few odds and ends, and she was setting her bin out front for collection. I was in two minds whether to stop and chat or not, especially considering the mood I was in, but in the end I did—something I'm now glad of.

During the conversation, she asked: *Who was that person, putting stuff through your letter box?*

When I asked who she meant, she told me that in the

last week she had twice seen a person deliver something. And both times, I'd been out.

Apparently, this person wasn't dressed too smartly, clad in old 'scraggy' clothes, according to her, and he walked with a noticeable limp. I asked what this person looked like, but she said she couldn't make out his face. Both times she'd been watching from her window, and her eyesight isn't what it was. On top of that, the mysterious person wore 'some kind of hooded top.' She confirmed that she'd seen him yesterday at around 6pm, roughly an hour before I'd returned home.

I didn't let on too much to Ms. Goddard. Firstly, because I didn't really know what to make of it, but mostly because I didn't want her involved in whatever this is.

I've been dwelling on what she told me for a few hours now and find that I am somewhat comforted by what the old lady has uncovered. That may sound a little counter-intuitive, as these letters are proof that someone is stalking and harassing me. But at least it is a *someone*.

It is a person.

One who has now been seen. And, from what I can guess, is not in any way supernatural.

Of course, to go to these extremes could well mean they are dangerous and unbalanced, something I am very concerned about, but at least I know what I'm dealing with. A person.

It could even be that he is the one who engineered everything that I and the others have witnessed so far. I can't fathom how, as yet, but surely it would be more plausible than the alternatives I've been considering?

This also led me to think more about the situation as a whole, and how this person could possibly be linked to Hobbes Hall. But so far I am drawing a blank.

I have emailed Chris and told him what I learned today. I feel he has a right to know, and maybe he can help me get to the bottom of this whole thing. After the scare he suffered the other day, which was my fault entirely, he deserves no less than some form of closure. As yet, I have heard nothing back from him.

I will write more tomorrow, when I have thought about this more.

~

It is 4.30am I have not slept well and now do not plan on going back to sleep at all.

Not tonight.

I awoke at roughly 3.00am, though I don't know what woke me. What I do know is that I had a horrible, unshakable feeling that I was being watched.

I tried to ignore this notion, but eventually was compelled to leave my bed, slide into my chair, and wheel myself to the bedroom window. As stupid as it sounds, I had the feeling someone was out there.

And I was right.

A figure was standing outside in the night, over the road from my home, next to Ms. Goddard's house. He—am sure it was a he—was looking up at me. The orange glow from the nearest streetlight put him in clear view, acting like a spotlight, and he was making no effort to hide himself. I could not see his face for the hood that he wore, but I was sure that this was the same person my neighbour had told me about.

Then, he did something. Even though I was trying to remain hidden below my sill, he clearly saw me. And he waved. Slowly and deliberately.

I wheeled away from the window in panic, not wanting to look at him any longer. However, once he was out of sight, I panicked even more, scared that he might decide, while out of sight, to run towards my front door and force himself inside.

So I looked out again, only to find he had gone.

Since then, my landline has rung three times, but I have not dared answer it. Instead, I have spent most of the last hour watching in fear from my window, waiting to see if he returns. I am scared, very scared. What I wrote about being relieved at this latest discovery was idiotic—a deranged psychopath would not get much of a struggle from man who cannot use his legs. I am debating calling the police.

And now my phone is ringing again.

1-14

12th August 2014

<No entry.>

1-15

13th August 2014

The reason for missing yesterday's entry was down to exhaustion. I slept most of the day and returned late.

But the day was a busy one, starting early in the morning when I received an email back from Chris. I have copied the email here:

∿

To: A.Clemintine5298@yahoo.co.uk
   From: Croona12@aol.com
   Subject: RE: Recent Developments
   Thanks for the update, Andrew. Don't really know what to make of it just yet. I think you should be careful, though. Whether this nutcase has something to with Hobbes Hall or not, you may want to consider reporting it to the police or something. It sounds like he's unbalanced, to say the least.
   Also, Kirsty and I have been doing some digging. She called me and told me she couldn't stop thinking about what happened

—something I can understand—and she wanted to know more about the place and maybe find something that could help explain it all. I tried contacting Steve as well, but no luck. Anyway, Kirsty and I travelled to Darlington, which is the nearest town to the hall, and went to the local library there. We spent the day digging up what we could. Andrew—we found some very strange shit!

I checked out what books we could and copied the rest of the information to paper. But it is way too much to put in an email.

You really need to see it for yourself. Any chance you can come over, or do you want us to get to you?

- Chris

∾

I called Chris immediately, telling him that I could get over that afternoon. He offered to travel to me instead—I sensed he felt a bit guilty about asking me to make the trip with my handicap—but after the previous night, I just wanted to get out of the house. He'd arranged for Kirsty to be present as well.

I had to take three different buses, and it took close to two hours, but every second I was out of the house felt like a relief.

When I arrived, I met Kirsty for the first time. She is very pretty and confident, and upon meeting her, I immediately felt pangs of guilt over my deceit.

We made a little small talk before getting down to business, and they showed me what they'd uncovered at the library: photocopies of archived newspapers, one or two old books regarding the local area, and some handwritten notes. There was too much to log here in one go, but I have copied a few key articles of interest:

~

Article from The County Chronicle. Local newspaper, now defunct. 18th June 1925.

Hobbes Hall Opens Its Doors.

Jubilation today as the much anticipated Hobbes Hall opened its doors to the public for the first time. The hall, a new sanatorium for tuberculosis and mental deficiency, is a beacon that highlights what our local area can achieve with people like Lord Hobbes pushing boundaries.

The privately owned, state-of-the-art facility will welcome its first residents tomorrow, and then, within its walls, healing can begin in earnest. Today, however, was a day for celebration. Local dignitaries attended the opening and were treated to refreshments, followed by a guided tour of some of the sanatorium, led by none other than owner and benefactor, Lord William Hobbes himself.

In his speech, Lord Hobbes shared his vision for the hall.

'For a long time, the good people of our region have lived with substandard facilities. Be it medical, social, or economic, we have had to work hard to progress in any area you could care to mention. Now, with Hobbes Hall, we have something that can be the envy of the country. Our equipment is of the highest order and our staff are leaders in their respective fields. We are proud to pioneer healing techniques not seen before in this country.'

Despite some unreasonable objections from a small minority, Hobbes hall is already an assured success, and signifies exciting times ahead.

~

Article from Northern Independent. Local newspaper, now defunct. 29th July 1927.

Terror at The Hall.

The problems at Hobbes Hall took a terrible turn for the worse last night as reports emerged of the attack, and murder, of an as-yet unnamed resident.

The facility has been plagued with problems from its very conception: public outcry at its proposed location, protests during construction, anger at its patient selection methods, and then the horror stories of sinister things practised within (all of which are passionately denied by the owner of the hall). These things should have been harbingers of worse to come.

We have now received reports that a patient in the mental deficiency ward escaped the confines of his room and managed to infiltrate the tuberculosis wing. The following may disturb, but we have been informed that he proceeded to then gut a patient being treated for tuberculosis, who subsequently died within an hour of the attack. It is also reported that the attacker himself was killed when staff attempted to restrain him.

William Hobbes, owner of the facility, is yet to comment.

Mr. Hobbes, 56, provoked outrage when he proposed the building of the facility in an area most seemed unsuitable, and too remote, for such a place. Not only that, Mr. Hobbes has a murky history, and is derided by many. He recently left the country for five years (some say he fled) to an unknown location.

It will be interesting to see how those who do defend this man and his ventures will respond to this latest tragic development.

∾

Excerpt from The Chapter. Local newspaper, now defunct. 17th August 1945.

Report by Trevor Chapman.

The police have finally called off their search for the missing Lord Hobbes, two years after his disappearance.

Hallelujah!

Call me heartless if you will, but if those rumours are to be believed, then his disappearance can only be seen as good news. Unfortunately, his eldest son is still around to pick up the pieces.

But surely they are just rumours, you say? A rumour, by its very nature, is unfounded.

Well, let's look at the facts.

The mortality rate at Hobbes Hall rivals that of a public morgue. Hobbes' own wife, admitted seven years ago, died within six months. Police have been called to the hall repeatedly, and they have more than one investigation currently ongoing regarding illegal procedures. Families of the deceased have been shouting at anyone who will listen that something is not right about that place.

Some people do choose to listen, but many turn a blind eye and deaf ear.

Why?

Well, the payroll of the Hobbes family is far reaching indeed, and even stretches to some, supposedly reputable, local newspapers.

I am among the many who know what it is like to lose some-body to that place. My cousin, Ernest Alderwood, was diagnosed with mental issues and, as his spouse was able to scrape together some funds, was admitted to Hobbes Hall. At first, visits were regular, and everything seemed in order, even if Ernest himself seemed a little more agitated than normal. We put that down to the new environment. Then, the visits became less frequent. Not because we did not want to see Ernest, but because the staff at Hobbes Hall continually blocked our visits with a variety of reasons and excuses, all of them medical jargon basically saying, 'He is too unwell.'

A year later, his partner received the message.

Ernest was dead.

He had apparently become violent and attacked a fellow patient, who fought back. Both died. As incredible as it sounds, this is the reason we were given. And then a police investigation validated their story.

Ernest had problems, but was never violent. If he did what they say, something happened to him to make *him that way. Something is inherently wrong with Hobbes Hall, and something needs to be done about it. I know I have written about this place in the past, and I know they may seem like the rantings of someone with a grudge (that may be), but I am not the only one who has lost a loved one to Hobbes Hall.*

If there is any justice, or if the new director of the facility has any sense of right and wrong, Hobbes Hall will be closed down immediately.

And forever.

∽

Excerpt from The Northern Echo. Local newspaper. 25th September 1997.

All but Forgotten Facility Closes Its Doors.

The St. Mary's care facility closed its doors yesterday after its last patient was transferred to a private care centre.

Formerly, and notoriously, known as Hobbes Hall, St. Mary's had been struggling financially for the best part of twenty years, limping along with substandard equipment and funds. The owner, Michael Hobbes—great grandson of founder William Hobbes—was left with little option but to close.

He has also filed for bankruptcy.

As reported last week, Michael's son, Jeremy, is currently on parole for an aggravated assault charge.

∽

We have uncovered plenty of interesting facts, to be sure, but what I really want to know more about is the hall's 'notoriety.'

So far, we have only snippets, and little else. But I am certain there is more to this—much more than we have been able to find. It was a lot to take in and, to be honest, I'm not sure if finding it out has done anything to ease my mind.

The place continues to consume my thoughts. Even though I've never been inside of it, I feel as though I know it well.

Sometimes I catch myself daydreaming of wandering its corridors. The thoughts soothe me... What the hell am I saying?

1-16

14th August 2014

I spoke with my neighbour, Ms. Goddard, again today. Not a chance meeting, she actually called around to my house to tell me that she saw that hooded man outside again last night. She said he just stood there, watching my house, for over an hour. She seemed concerned for me and asked if I knew who it was. I just said that I didn't know.

But it was what she told me next that I found most troubling. Ms. Goddard had grown annoyed at his lurking and rattled her window, with the intent of telling him to 'get lost'(her words). She told me how he then turned to face her, with his head cocked to one side. But instead of seeing his face, all she could make out were dirty bandages, wrapped around his head, with eye holes crudely cut into the material. She told me he just stared at her for a while until he finally walked away.

It had obviously given her a fright, as she was still a little shaken when she relayed the story.

I haven't told Chris or Kirsty about this as of yet. I'm sure I will, but for now I don't really know what to do.

1-17

15th August 2014

Steve is missing.

Chris rang today and told me he called round to see Steve. He'd been worried after not hearing from him since the trip to that damn hall. Chris had tried to get in touch a number of times with no response, so yesterday he went to Steve's flat. Initially, no one was there.

That in itself wouldn't have worried Chris. Steve could easily just have been out at the time of calling; however, as Chris was about to leave, he bumped into Steve's girlfriend, Julie.

She had called around to check on Steve as well. Apparently she'd not been able to get in contact with him for the past three days, either. She had a key, and so Chris was able to get inside the flat with her.

He told me that there was a build-up of mail on the entrance mat, but no sign of Steve. Julie was understandably upset and explained that Steve had been acting very strangely recently, to the point of almost becoming a recluse.

He had previously told her a little about the trip to Hobbes Hall, but had left her in the dark on most of the details. She said he'd been as scared as she'd ever known him. Julie tried to get some information out of Chris about what had happened, but Chris didn't feel comfortable involving her, so he lied.

I can't blame him for that. I seem to have done a lot of it myself.

My hope is that Steve got spooked and fled to a relative's, or something like that. I know how much that place can get inside your head and take over your thoughts. However, deep down, I fear something has happened to him.

Something bad.

I worry for him, which is strange, as I've never even met the man.

But then, I guess the real reason I worry for him is because if something has indeed happened, then I know it is my fault. And it could happen to me, too.

1-18

16th August 2014

Dear God, things are getting worse.

Ms. Goddard is dead.

Murdered.

The police have been questioning me about it to see if I know anything, and I told them about the hooded person who has been watching me. I have to go to the station now to give a full statement and answer more questions. I have no idea if I should tell them about Hobbes Hall. Would I sound crazy? Would it implicate me somehow?

Christ, I don't know what to do.

1-19

17th August 2014

The visit to the police station was exhausting.

They are now on the lookout for the hooded figure I told them about, though they have no reports of anyone else in the street seeing him. I didn't mention anything about the hall. It all seems too... I don't know, crazy?

They also told me how Ms. Goddard died. I suspect they did this to provoke some kind of reaction from me.

Her stomach had been crudely cut from navel to chest with a large shard of glass. The glass had come from the rear window of her home, which the attacker had broken to gain entry. Ms. Goddard had been bound and gagged and left alone, bleeding out as the injuries slowly took her life.

I'm scared. Horrified. I feel frightened and helpless and I fucking hate it!

I emailed Chris to tell him what happened (couldn't bring myself to phone him and speak about it). I haven't heard back.

It's late, past midnight, and I know I will not sleep well

tonight. I can't remember the last time I slept properly, to be honest. I keep wanting to look from my bedroom window, just to make sure that hooded bastard isn't there. But, at the same time, I'm too terrified to look.

And yet, through it all, I still feel a yearning to return to that damn place. The pull is becoming ever stronger.

And that is fucking insane. I sometimes feel like I'm losing my mind.

I'll try to sleep again tonight, but I know that if I do, it will be restless, filled with dreams and nightmares of that place. Of its rooms and corridors, and of its patients and its past. And of that horrifying, unknowable thing that exists in the dark and the shadows. The thing behind it all.

And I will dream of that other place, too. The one beneath and beyond Hobbes Hall. The living nightmare with terrors so unfathomable they would tear apart human sanity.

Christ, I don't even know what I'm writing anymore!!!!

1-20

18th August 2014

I am at Chris' house again. I've been here since early morning. He picked me up just before dawn, after I called him in a blind panic.

I've brought my laptop with me, which I am using to write up this journal. I don't really know why I keep it going, but getting everything down seems to give me some kind of respite from the fear.

Because when I woke up this morning, after only two hours of sleep, there was something waiting for me on my pillow.

Next to my head. It was wrapped in faded yellow paper and was heavily stained brown.

I opened it.

God only knows why.

Inside, I found something that was red, wet, and glistening. I'm no doctor, but I know it had been cut and removed from inside of someone. What part or organ, exactly, I have no idea. I do know who it was taken from, though. At least, I can give a reasonable guess: the poor old woman who is dead because of me.

Ms. Goddard.

I know I should have gone to the police with this, but I couldn't. I'm scared—scared that doing so could cause something worse to happen to me. And scared, also, that it would implicate me somehow.

I know it sounds stupid, and paranoid and selfish, but I guess that's my state of mind at the minute.

Chris is also showing signs of the panic I'm feeling, more so than I've seen from him before. We haven't told Kirsty about this, and I don't think we're going to. Chris has said I can stay here for as long as I need to and, had it not been for the police being involved, I think I would take him up on his offer for quite a while. But how would it look if I ran from my home? I would be incriminated for certain.

Still, I am in no rush to get back to my house after what I found this morning, so I will stay here for tonight and return home tomorrow.

This is all so fucked up.

1-21

Chris wants to go back to the hall.

He told me this morning, the words pouring out of him as if they had been pent up inside for some time.

I don't know why he wants to, and I'm trying to talk him out of it, but he is insistent. He seems to think that it's the only way to get to the bottom of what's going on. To put a stop to everything that's happening.

He also said that, since he went to the hall, he's seen some hooded person standing outside of his house at night, watching him. Just as I have.

I've convinced Chris not to do anything too rash just yet, but I'm not sure how long I can keep him at bay. No matter how he reasons it, I get the impression his need to return to that place is not natural. It's something he is battling with.

And it seems we are both struggling with the same issue. So we need to be strong for each other.

But he asked, if he does go back, would I want to go with him. The question gave me pause, but I said no. What does he expect of me? I told him no good would come of going back there. And I couldn't exactly do much in my condition.

As much as I don't want to, I'm getting ready to return home. God only knows what I'm going to find this time. Will write more soon to help try to make sense of my muddled thoughts.

❧

It's been such a long day. When Chris first brought me home, everything appeared to be just as I'd left it. No nasty surprises.

Until I checked my answer phone.

There was a message from an unknown caller. I played it on the loudspeaker when Chris was still with me. Even before listening, I knew it would be bad. And it was. We both listened, and Chris seemed to share my feeling of foreboding.

The recording itself started off with the same static I'd heard from previous calls, but the static soon faded, and we could then hear breathing. In the background, there was a muffled whining of someone in pain. Then, a voice—hoarse and excitable—said:

'We miss you, Andrew. You and your friends. Come and see us. We want to show you things. One of your friends is here with us now. We are showing him glimpses of heaven. And your friend screams his wondrous approval.'

Then, the message ended. But it set Chris off again.

He insisted that we go back to the hall, convinced this 'friend' mentioned was Steve. I tried to calm him down, saying it was probably some kind of trick, but he got more heated and animated. The more I tried to talk him out of it, the angrier he got. In the end, he started screaming at me, calling me a 'fucking coward,' and saying it was my fault that everyone was mixed up in this mess in the first place.

Then he stormed out.

A little later, Kirsty called me, saying she'd been speaking to Chris and he'd told her that he was going to go back to the hall. He wouldn't tell her much more than that, but she knew something had happened, and she demanded I tell her what.

At first, I tried to act ignorant of the whole thing. But Kirsty saw straight through that and became even more insistent. I broke down and told her about the message, how it mentioned 'a friend,' and Chris' plans to go back. She was, understandably, a little shaken by this, but said she wanted to come over to hear the message for herself.

When Kirsty arrived, I played it to her. I offered my explanation—that I thought it was some kind of trick. Not necessarily a prank, but more a way to lure us back to Hobbes Hall.

Kirsty asked if there was anything else I wasn't telling her. I think it was because I felt a little safer having someone here with me—instead of being alone and scared all the time—that I broke down and told her everything. About the hooded person that's been stalking me, what happened to Ms. Goddard, and what I'd found waiting for me when I woke up yesterday. I was actually in tears as I unloaded all of this information. If Kirsty was shaken before, she was terrified now.

But she insisted we stop Chris.

Kirsty tried phoning him again, even though I already had, but got no response. The calls just rang out.

So she demanded we go to Hobbes Hall ourselves, to find him and bring him back.

Though I was torn, and part of me wanted to return to the hall (and not just to help Chris), I ultimately said no.

Kirsty was disgusted with me and said that I was a coward. The second time I heard that in the same day.

It was accurate.

So, Kirsty went alone.

I haven't heard from her all night (it's approaching midnight as I write this). I've tried calling—both her and Chris—but the calls just ring out.

I feel low, gutless, and torn.

And I'm exhausted. I'm going to turn in and see what my dreams have in store for me tonight.

1-22

20th August 2014

My mind betrays me. I think I may be going crazy.

Somehow, that place has a link to me. Whatever is happening there, it seems to have infected my subconscious. Whether that is from my two fleeting visits, I can't be sure, but the link is there.

I will describe the dream I had last night. The most vivid yet. Some part of me feels that it wasn't just a dream, but something else. A vision? A message? Events that actually happened?

I don't know.

But in the dream, I was in Hobbes Hall. It was night, and the hall was as I remember it in my previous dreams: dark, dingy, and abandoned, with paint peeling from the walls and empty halls. It was quiet.

But then it wasn't.

The same screams I heard the first time I'd found the place thundered through the building. Screams of absolute agony and anguish.

But there were other cries too: cries of passion, of elation, of ecstasy. While some voices sounded like they were suffering, others seemed to be revelling. Was this the sound of the tormentors?

I wandered the halls, not in my chair, not even in my body, just floating wherever I wanted to go. I remember feeling terrified but compelled to go on. Despite the crescendo of agony and pain all around, I found no one.

At first. Until I descended to the basement.

The ceiling there was low, and the environment pitch black. And then, there was light, a dull yellow hue coming from ahead. A figure was sitting beneath this glow, restrained to a chair, completely bound with rope.

I carried on, getting closer. The light turned out to be from a single bulb hanging from the ceiling.

Blood stained the figure's familiar clothes, and his head was tightly wrapped in crimson-soaked bandages.

I wanted to unwrap these bandages, to confirm my suspicions, but I could not, for I was completely disembodied. But another figure then stepped into view, one I remember seeing from my bedroom window. The same person who killed my neighbour. He, as if knowing what I wanted to see, unwrapped the bandages.

As expected, I saw Chris, but the skin had been peeled from his face. He started to scream.

The figure that stood beside Chris then started to talk to me, his voice muffled by his own dirtied bandages.

The man simply said that I was to return to Hobbes Hall, that I was being called, and that I could not ignore the call any longer. And he promised that when I returned, I would be shown things beyond my understanding. He pointed to a large trap door set in the concrete floor. On top of this trap door, sat an object—triangular, about half a foot high, and jet black. Yet I could see, or sense, something shift beneath the surface.

'*Down there,*' the mysterious man told me.

Then I heard fresh sounds. Noises so horrific that I couldn't comprehend what could be making them. Animal, monster, something more? It was indescribable, but it seemed infinitely powerful.

Panic rose in me, then I woke… and the bandaged man was standing in the corner of my room, watching me.

I was certain he was there to kill me, but instead he talked, as he had in the dream, as if what he was saying was somehow a continuation of the message he had started in my sub-conscious, picking up where he left off. His voice was even more strained and muffled than in my dream.

He told me he that he is a descendant of William Hobbes, and that his family is forever tied to that place. It is his home, even though it is now abandoned by the living.

But, he said, it is not empty. Something resides there. Something William Hobbes uncovered and set loose. This thing had claimed the very souls of the damned that were once committed to Hobbes Hall. William Hobbes, too, he said, went willingly to it.

When I asked what this thing was, he simply told me it was a God. A real God, not like the make-believe one much of the world now believes in. Real Gods do not exist and function like the world today would have us believe, he said. The place this thing is from—it's Heaven—is pure chaos and terror, and filled with things beyond our understanding. But, he continued, by giving himself over to it, even a little, and doing its bidding, the man is apparently allowed a glimpse of its forbidden knowledge.

He told me that this knowledge—and gaining more of it

—is more precious to him than breath. And he then told me that he can offer me the same.

The thing that lives there has noticed me, and it wants me for its own. The man said it was unavoidable, and that I would go there of my own free will... eventually. Down beneath the surface.

To the belly of the beast.

When finished with his message, the man simply turned and left. That was over four hours ago. I'm still terrified.

And yet...

I know what I'm going to do. The fear is fading a little. It is being replaced by something else.

The knowledge he spoke of sounds... enticing.

1-23

21st August 2014

This is to be my last entry. I'm going home!

I tried calling both Chris and Kirsty again. I don't know why I tried Chris, given that I knew what had happened to him. And, perhaps trying to get hold of Kirsty was a way to say goodbye to my old life. Regardless, I got hold of neither at first. But, around lunch time, while trying Chris' phone again, I got an answer. But it wasn't Chris.

It was *him*.

He again beckoned me and again promised me that hidden knowledge. The forbidden truth. I yearned for it.

I told him I was coming.

The joy I feel at accepting this is indescribable. Finally, my existence will have meaning.

Perhaps, one day, someone will find this record, and glean some kind of understanding of what happened to me from it. Perhaps they can follow me to the paradise that awaits me. A place not of this world.

I hope so.

I ready myself to leave and know I will never return. I am heading off to my ascension, and yet I cannot wait.

In truth, I can still feel part of my mind screaming against me, fighting to be heard. But that part of me grows ever more quiet. Soon it will be silent forever.

Farewell.

1-24

22nd August 2014

<No entry.>

Postface
by Dr. Addington

My own investigations turned up a little further information.

On the 15th of January 2015, two bodies were removed from the abandoned hall.

The first was the body of a Mr. Christopher Daniels. He was found bound to a chair in the basement, and he had been stripped of the skin from his face. The body of a girl, Kirsty Johnston, was also found.

And that was it.

The only thing I can find out about the author, one Andrew Clementine, is that he has been missing for a number of years.

I have decided not to hand this information over to the police. After all, what can be done now? There is no trace of Andrew, or the mysterious bandaged man chronicled in this diary, and I can only guess as to where they are now.

It may be that they have gone, or been taken, to this

'Heaven' that Andrew hints at in his diary. It is this other place that consumes me and my work.

A curse handed down to me by my family.

It was my great grandfather who first discovered the existence of this place, and its secret has been passed down to me. One I guard but devote my life to.

I have no choice but to find out more. The secrets and knowledge consume me.

I know others are aware of it too. I now have become aware of an organisation, or cult, that worships this 'other place,' and some of its entities. I fear they know much more than I do, and this fact tempts me to make contact with them, dangerous as that may be.

Also, I have further leads to pursue. I have arranged to meet a girl who has recently been through quite a traumatic event. She is the sole survivor of an encounter with a family of cannibals, if it can be believed. And while these lunatics would usually not offer me anything more than a professional curiosity, it is the end of the story, as she tells it, that interests me.

She also has in her possession a book that will be of great interest to me.

Most have branded her crazy, and a liar, and because of that, the book she has in her possession has not been shared with anyone. Which is fortunate for me. From the small amount I have found out from her, I think this case will be fascinating.

I have also seen stories of a tragic event in the North East of England, and some strange happenings regarding a rumoured asylum that practiced certain insidious procedures. Once I have spoken with the lady who escaped the cannibals, I shall pursue these cases as well.

Despite all the knowledge that has been passed down to

me, and despite everything I have discovered myself, I still feel like I know next to nothing about the mysterious 'other world' that consumes me, though I am certain of its existence.

Is it another dimension, or something else? The endless questions, that only prompt further questions, are maddening.

- Dr. Phillip Addington, 2019.

THE LATE SHIFT

2-1

'Quiet night again,' Jack Collings said to his partner while rubbing the base of his neck with his bony fingers. His back was sore from being trapped in this police car for well over an hour. Another late shift that would no doubt drag through until the early hours of the morning.

Just sitting. Waiting. With nothing to do.

His partner, Andrew Todd, sat behind the wheel adjacent to him and nodded his head in agreement. 'Most nights are nowadays,' he said.

Jack sipped his black coffee from the cardboard cup. The two police officers had stopped at a large, well-known franchise in order to kill some time, but it wasn't Jack's preferred brand of coffee. He preferred the ground beans of smaller coffee shops, but finding one open at this time of night would be impossible. He pulled in another long gulp of the bitter liquid.

Not perfect, but not terrible. It would certainly do.

Jack looked over to Andrew, who was staring out of the windshield ahead, seemingly at nothing in particular. The dark street beyond them was quiet and completely devoid of life, save for the two of them sitting here in the idle car. Normally on a quiet night like tonight, they would have been chatting and shooting the shit, but Andrew seemed pre-occupied.

And Jack had a feeling he knew why.

Jack had started working with Andrew just under a year ago, and he knew that today marked the one-year anniversary of his last partner's disappearance. Whether the man was alive or dead now, no one really knew. Assumed dead, of course, because Trevor Atkins had left behind a wife and two young children that he had absolutely adored. And those that knew him knew there was little chance of him just running away to abandon them.

'See the game last night?' Jack asked in a poor attempt to force conversation.

'Missed it,' Andrew replied, with no further comment— eyes still focused on the dead street ahead, thoughts clearly somewhere else.

Jack prayed for their radio to suddenly burst into life with a call out. Anything would do, just to get them both doing something. Perhaps it would help to pull Andrew out of his funk. Andrew was normally a happy-go-lucky type of guy, but tonight he was withdrawn and cold. Jack debated bringing up Trevor, if only to try and get his partner—and friend—to talk about the whole situation. But every time he had tried in the past, he'd been cut down.

Don't want to talk about that.

Tonight, with things clearly more raw than usual, Jack decided against it, feeling that waiting in uncomfortable silence for their shift to end was the better option.

But, to his surprise, that was not what Andrew wanted.

'A year today,' he said out of the blue. His voice was almost robotic.

Jack didn't know how to respond at first, and the only thing he could think to do was to nod in agreement and offer a feeble, 'Yeah.'

A few moments of silence. 'Jack?' Andrew asked, but didn't wait for a response before carrying on. 'What do you know about that night?'

Yet again, Jack was caught off guard. It was not a question he was expecting, but he answered truthfully. 'Not much,' he said. 'I don't think many people know much, to be honest. Trevor's wife reported that he took a private call in the middle of the night—from a number that turned out to be from a burner phone which was never found or traced—and told her he had to go and that he would be back soon. He left and he was never seen again.'

'Anything else?'

A shrug from Jack. 'As far as I know, nothing else turned up. The guys investigating looked into his background to see if there was anything untoward going on, but didn't find anything. Whoever was on the phone with Trevor that night was involved, no doubt, but that person is a mystery. A ghost.'

'And the reports of sightings of Trevor?'

Jack nodded. 'Of his car heading out of town? Sure.'

'Towards that old industrial estate,' Andrew confirmed.

Jack frowned and pressed his palms against the hot cup in his hands. He suddenly had an idea where this was going. 'Doesn't mean he went *there*. He could have just kept going. That road leads to the next town over as well.'

'But it does takes you up that way,' Andrew calmly argued. 'And there isn't anyone up there anymore. The place isn't in use. Lot of buildings just standing empty.'

'I know. And they were all searched. The estate might not be in use anymore, but there is still security at the perimeter. None of the guards saw him up there, and the search didn't turn anything up, either.'

Andrew nodded. 'That's true. But there are a lot of stories about that place.'

'Don't,' Jack snapped, but regretted it immediately. He should have been more diplomatic to a guy who was clearly struggling. Even so, he didn't like where Andrew was going with this and was surprised his partner would take the conversation in that direction. Andrew didn't seem like the type of person to believe in ghost stories.

'Bad accident there in eighty-two,' Andrew went on. 'How many dead? And how many died or went missing before that?'

'It was just an accident,' Jack stressed. 'Yes, a lot of people died, but it has become apparent that health and safety were pretty shitty back then.'

'That doesn't account for everything. Or the stories since, either.'

Jack shook his head. He had heard the stories, of course —everyone in town had; they were local legends—but they were all bullshit. Stories used to scare kids. Surely Andrew could see that?

Both men remained silent for a short while, before Andrew eventually carried on. 'I need to ask something of you. And it doesn't sound like you are going to like it.'

Jack turned to his partner. 'What?'

'I want to go out to that place. Now. Tonight. I need to search it.'

Jack couldn't help his jaw from dropping open. 'You're nuts,' he shot back, shaking his head.

Andrew gave a sad smile. And for the first time since they had gotten in the car that night, turned to look at Jack.

'Please.'

Andrew was a large man, six-two and heavyset. Like a gorilla. He had a broad, creased brow, and dark hair that only further added to his ape-like appearance. He dwarfed Jack, too, who himself was lean and just under five-nine. But Andrew was also a gentle giant... usually. When he needed to, he could summon all the strength he had, and it was an awesome thing to behold. Jack knew that if Andrew wanted to, he was more than capable of just dragging Jack out there.

But Andrew wasn't doing that. He was asking, nicely. And the sound of his voice—almost pleading for help—stabbed at Jack's heart.

'Andrew,' Jack started, trying to find the best way to let his friend down. 'We're on duty. We can't just go up there for a snoop around.'

'If we get a call, we drop it,' Andrew promised.

'We won't find anything. It's been a year. What do you hope—'

'Look,' Andrew interrupted, 'I know how this sounds. But there is a reason I want to go up there. A good reason. But I need your help to do it.'

Jack squinted his eyes. 'What's the reason?'

Andrew took a deep breath. 'I got a call. Earlier today. From a withheld number. It was a guy, said if I wanted to know more about what happened, then I need to go up to the industrial estate on the edge of town. Tonight. But no back-up. And he said I couldn't tell anyone.'

'It's a joke,' Jack shot back, as if it was the most obvious thing in the world. 'Some sick fucker is—'

'It was Trevor,' Andrew cut in, stunning Jack into silence. Andrew went on. 'And don't tell me it wasn't. We were part-ners for six years. I know that man's voice. It was him. And he needed my help.'

Jack studied the larger man's face and found nothing but

sincerity. And, even, a little fear—something Jack was not used to seeing from Andrew. 'Are you sure?' he asked.

'I'm certain,' Andrew replied with conviction.

Jack wasn't sure he believed that. He didn't question that Andrew believed it, but Jack could not accept that Trevor would go missing for so long—leaving his family behind—and just call like that out of the blue. 'Then we need to call it in,' Jack said, eventually. 'Shit, you should have alerted someone, Andrew. We could have had people up there searching that place already.'

'Call came just before my shift started. Trevor was adamant that I not tell anyone. He sounded like he was scared, Jack. Look, I know how this sounds, and I'm sorry for dropping it on you, but what was I supposed to do?'

Jack sighed. 'So, if this... Trevor... was adamant you tell no one, why tell me?'

Andrew looked down to his large, fidgeting hands, which were picking at already painfully short nails. 'Because I don't know what else to do. I couldn't exactly get up there without you tonight, given we are on shift together, other than bolting and leaving you. And... I don't know what I'm going to find up there. I'm just worried. Look, if we go, we can just skirt the perimeter. And if there are two of us, it's easier to call something in if the shit hits the fan. I know I'm asking a lot, and you are free to tell me to go fuck myself, but I have to go up there, Jack. I *need* to know.'

Jack rubbed a hand over his face, feeling torn. He knew he should be taking Andrew up on the offer to tell him to go fuck himself. And then he should call it in. That was the correct thing to do, he knew—the sensible thing to do. Hell, any other decision considering the fucking craziness of what Andrew was saying would be downright stupid.

But Jack already knew what his answer was going to be.

A stupid one. He knew it when he'd first seen the pleading look on the face of a man who had saved his life twice already in the space of a year. The same man who he now counted as a good friend, as well as a partner.

Jack was going to help Andrew.

He could argue and lament for a little if it made him feel better—and he certainly felt like doing so—but, in the end, his answer would be the same. So, Jack relented. His head dropped back to the headrest of the seat and he sighed.

'Fuck me,' he said. 'You aren't asking much, are you?'

'I know,' Andrew replied. 'And like I said, feel free—'

'Let's get this over with,' Jack cut in.

'Really?' Andrew asked, eyebrows rising and a genuine note of surprise in his voice. The man didn't smile, given there wasn't much to smile about, but he did look a little relieved. 'Thank you,' he said. 'I really mean it. Thank you.'

Jack waved a dismissive hand. 'Don't thank me. Just take the fall if we get in trouble. And buy me a shit-load of whiskey.'

Andrew nodded, starting the engine and putting the car into gear. 'Done.'

The car pulled forward and set off towards the old, abandoned industrial estate on the outskirts of the town.

What the fuck have I just agreed to?

Jack had only ever been up this way once before—to disperse an unruly gang of kids—and that had been during the day, when things looked distinctly less ominous.

Now, as they sat just outside of a chain-link fence and entry gate, in the pitch black of night, it looked like a different place completely. Security lighting shone up the height of some of the towering structures of twisted metal and girders. Steel chimneys that would have once belched out God-knows-what still towered in the sky, wrapped in a criss-cross of walkways and scaffolding.

Jack had no idea what these units were, or what their purposes had originally been. There were four main structures in total, the tallest being one of the central of the four. All were menacing and seemed to emit a cold, unclean, and oppressive energy. The buildings' once silver finishes had now rusted to dirty browns and yellows, and the structures were all a mismatch of huge drums, towers, steel beams, and branching cables.

While Jack was sure they had once been designed for a function, and no doubt performed it well, to him the buildings—if they could be described as such—resembled little more than huge piles of junk metal and concrete that had been fused chaotically together.

The units all stood centrally on a broken and pock-marked concrete base that stretched out for many metres in either direction. Huts and smaller buildings, dwarfed by these towering alien masters, were scattered about a yard that ran to the perimeter security fencing. Entrance gates blocked off the access road beyond—the very one Jack and Andrew were now parked on. The gate ahead of them should have been secured, but the lock that bound them together lay on the floor, and one of the gates had been pulled inward, now open a few inches.

A small, wooden security hut sat to the side of this gate, just inside the fence. It stood empty. That was something Jack had noticed immediately as they stopped the car.

'Maybe the guard is carrying out a patrol or something?' Andrew offered.

'Could be,' Jack agreed. 'But why has the gate been left open like that? I don't like it.' Jack then heard the sound of the driver's side door to the car open. 'What are you doing?' he asked as Andrew began to disembark.

'You can wait here if you want,' Andrew said. 'I'm going to have a quick look around. It's what we came up here for, after all.'

But, just as Jack knew he wasn't going to let Andrew come up here alone, he wasn't going to let his partner go off wandering by himself.

'Fuck,' he snapped, under his breath. And then got out as well.

Though it was summer, the air was cold, and a sharp contrast to the heated interior of the car. Jack adjusted his stab vest—which had ridden up after he'd been sitting down for so long—and walked to the front of the car to join Andrew. The two of them looked out over the sprawling complex.

It was quiet, very quiet, and Jack wasn't sure if that was necessarily out of the ordinary, given this place was no longer used, but it made him uneasy, regardless. He wasn't used to such total silence.

The quiet was soon broken, however, as Andrew strode forward and pushed open the security gate; the prolonged screech of protesting metal as the gate slid open was exacerbated by the absence of any other sound, making it seem unnaturally loud and drawn out.

Now inside the compound, Jack wanted to check something.

'Hold on,' he said and walked over to the security hut.

The unit was small, with just enough space to house a small desk, a seat, and a filing cabinet. A computer and monitor sat on the desk, and on the monitor's screen, Jack could see a four-way split image, each one evidently a view from a different security camera, all presumably from somewhere inside the industrial units. All four images showed different corridors. Each view was elevated—close to the ceiling—and looked down nondescript concrete hallways. Each shot radiated with the green hue of night-vision.

There didn't seem to be any movement in the security images but, after a few moments, the screen flickered, and then four different views were shown, replacing the previous ones. Jack realised that the system was one that cycled through the different cameras mounted around the grounds. He continued to watch as the cycling continued, showing a plethora of different corridors and rooms within the different structures, each set of four staying on screen for about thirty seconds. In the bottom corner of each view, a heading showed the location of the shot. The top left was always Building 1, and it changed its sub-headings with each change of the cameras. Hallway 1, then Plant Room, then Basement, and so on. The top right was Building 2, bottom left Building 3, and bottom right was Building 4.

'See anything?' Andrew asked. He was still standing outside of the hut—given there was not room for them both inside—and was peering in through the open door.

'No,' Jack said, 'can't see a thing.'

Then the view quickly snapped to fullscreen, and Jack jumped back at what he saw. It was a different camera shot this time, one he had not seen before, with the heading Building 2: Hallway 4. But the fullscreen shot was filled with the lower half of a face, so close to the camera that anything above the nose was out of shot. Even though the camera display was low resolution, Jack could still make out that the skin of the face was horribly blistered and bloody, creased with the wrinkles and lines of very advanced age. Thin lips pulled back into a smile, revealing cracked and black teeth, and a stream of liquid ran from the nose.

'Who the fuck is that?' Jack asked. The image then cut to static, and blinking text popped up, displaying the words: Unable to Connect.

'Someone is in there,' Andrew stated. 'And I don't think it is the security guard.'

'If it was,' Jack added, 'then he wasn't in a good way. Did you see the state of his face? What the fuck happened to him?'

A sinking feeling developed in Jack's gut, as the view on the monitor flicked back to one of the four-way shots, only this time every camera showed the same static and the same message as the previous screen: Unable to Connect.

Jack was about to turn to his partner to suggest calling it

in, because in truth Jack had already seen enough to unsettle him. However, Andrew was looking elsewhere.

'Look,' Andrew said, pointing to the main entrance door to one of the central units. It was a fair distance away, but when focusing, Jack could clearly see the main door was open. And, what's more, a figure stood in the doorway, cloaked in black. Its face hidden.

'Hello?' Andrew yelled over. In response, the mysterious person simply stepped back, vanishing into the darkness inside. Andrew suddenly began to march over.

'Hey,' Jack shouted, jogging after his partner. 'Where the hell do you think you're going?'

'To see what's going on,' Andrew said, not stopping, and shrugging off Jack's half-hearted attempt to grab his arm.

'I don't think that is a good idea,' Jack stated. 'We should radio for back-up, then go in.'

'Not until we know what's going on.'

'This is stupid,' Jack stressed. 'Just stop and think.'

'You stop and think,' Andrew shot back, his eyes still focused on the building ahead. His pace did not slow. 'I'm going in.'

Jack wasn't psychic, and he didn't believe in precognition, or any of that rubbish, but he knew to listen to his gut when something didn't feel right.

And this didn't feel right.

Even so, knowing he could not deter Andrew, Jack realised he had only two options: wait out here and call for back-up while Andrew went inside, or go in with his friend and lend back-up and support of his own.

Jack cursed himself as he followed the larger man towards the building, drawing out his torch to penetrate the dark as they crossed the threshold.

This is fucking stupid, Jack told himself as they both cast their beams about the space in which they now found themselves. It was a rather basic reception area, with a simple desk on which sat a dusty old sign-in book. The room was roughly square and contained only the desk and four steel doors set into the walls, all of them painted a dull green.

One of the doors was open.

'There,' Andrew said, pointing towards the open door, and he set off through it. Jack could do nothing but follow, aware that this could be one of those times in life where it did not pay to be so loyal.

'We need to slow down and think about what the fuck we're doing,' Jack barked. He was fast losing patience with his partner, and any sympathy he felt for the man's situation would only stretch so far.

But Andrew just ignored him.

The concrete corridor they were heading down ended with a set of double doors, which were, again, wide open. They led into a more open area, and the beams from the flashlights showed a low ceiling that was lined with thick, aluminium ducts and black cables. Machinery and control units were scattered around the room—complete with pressure gauges, dials, buttons, display panels, and other things that completely confused Jack. He was reminded of movies where killer cyborgs stalked heroines through such industrial backdrops. There was even a large industrial press, and Jack's damned imagination flashed to an image of him lying in it as the unstoppable metal ceiling slowly came down to crush his organs.

He shook his head, expelling the image, and was about to insist that they get the hell out of there. But instead, they both heard a shriek of pain that echoed from deeper within the building somewhere. Jack's body seized up, but silence soon returned. No further cries could be heard.

'Enough,' Jack said, and reached for the radio that was clasped to the left-hand side of his upper chest. He pushed down the communication button and spoke into it. 'Dispatch, come in.' He waited a few moments, but was not met with a response. He tried again. 'Dispatch, are you picking this up?' Still nothing. He twisted a dial, turning up the volume, and communicated again. Then Jack listened intently, but again there was no response. 'Fucking thing,' he snapped and gave it a smack. He was about to try again when a deafening burst of static sounded from the radio, making him jump.

'What the fuck is wrong with it?' Andrew asked, turning his head away from the noise, which only increased in volume and intensity. Jack removed the radio from his chest and held it in front of him, shaking the device. When that didn't work, he moved to turn it off, but the static suddenly died down. It didn't vanish completely, but the ferocity was greatly reduced.

However, just as the cracking noise threatened to die out completely, another sound could be heard from the electronic device.

Sobbing.

The voice seemed feminine, and the sniffling came in short, sharp breaths. Jack and Andrew cast each other confused looks. Jack knew that these radios should only be able to make contact with Dispatch, and this muffled whimpering sure as hell wasn't coming from there.

So who was it?

'Hello?' Jack said into the radio, while pressing down on

the push-to-talk button, which would allow his voice to transmit.

The sobbing slowed. Then a hoarse voice responded to him. '*It... hurts. It... hurts.*'

Then the screaming began.

So sharp and loud that it caused Jack to drop his radio to the floor and cover his ears. Andrew had a similar reaction and took a few steps back. The man's mouth moved, and Jack could read the words that formed on his lips—*What the fuck?*—though he could hear nothing above the harsh screeching.

As quickly as it started, the cacophony of cracking wails suddenly ceased, leaving them in a silence so sudden it took a moment to register. Eventually Jack removed his hands from his ears, which were still ringing, then looked to Andrew again.

Silence. No sound could be heard at all, which was a harsh contrast to the thunderous screaming that almost deafened them only moments ago.

Jack stared at the discarded radio that lay on the floor between him and Andrew.

'What the hell was that?' Jack asked.

Andrew could only shake his head. 'I have no fucking idea.'

It was enough for Jack to call a halt to this whole thing. It was too much. They should have been gone from here before they'd even entered the building. He'd done his part and tried to help his friend and partner as best he could—gone out on a limb for him—but now things had taken a turn that he couldn't explain, and Jack's gut told him things were only going to get worse. So it was time to put an end to this charade and get the hell out of there. Enough was enough.

'We're leaving,' he stated, grabbing the radio from the ground. 'Let's go.'

'But—'

However, this time, Jack wasn't listening. He raised a dismissive hand and turned and walked off. 'Not interested, Andrew. Come on.'

Thankfully, he heard Andrew coming after him, and Jack made his way quickly back down the corridor they had just emerged from. While he wasn't quite jogging, Jack was walking very quickly. That voice on the radio had definitely creeped him out, and he felt a cold shiver run down his spine and arms. Though he didn't stop to check, he knew goosebumps had also formed on his skin.

But Jack didn't get far.

He stopped in his tracks when the beam from the torch-light illuminated something up ahead. Andrew quickly came to a stop behind him, as well. Neither said a word, they just took in the sight of this figure—shrouded in a black hood and robes—as it stood motionless, arms crossed at the waist, each hand disappearing within the opposite sleeve of the loose, dark material.

The bad feeling in Jack's gut only intensified.

Was this the person that had contacted Andrew and drawn him here tonight? Trevor, Andrew's old partner? Or someone else?

Jack looked to Andrew, but the big man offered nothing in return, simply staring ahead at the mysterious figure, his expression unreadable.

'Hello?' Jack called, keeping the beam of light trained on the mysterious stranger. A hood from the robes obscured most of the person's face and hung low below the brow, as the head was bowed forward. Jack could, however, just about make out a mouth and jaw, though the pale skin looked... odd, and streaked with red. 'Who are you?' Jack asked.

As expected, he got no response. Then Jack focused on the exposed part of the face that he could see, studying it as best he could from this distance and squinting his eyes to get better focus. Jack soon realised what it was that looked so odd about the skin. Blotches on the flesh, he realised, and painful-looking blisters. The red streaks were blood.

This was the person he had seen on the security footage out in the hut, before all of the cameras went dead.

Then the person moved—raising up a hand and extending a long, bony figure towards them. Jack wasn't sure if the stranger was pointing at them, or behind them, and he quickly turned his head and the torch to look back, but could see nothing of note. He cast his gaze back to the stranger, who was still pointing.

What is this person trying to say?

Soon enough, however, the message became clear, spoken by a voice that seemed to emanate not from the figure ahead, but from the very air around them, booming out in a distorted and gravelly tone.

'*Turn back!*'

And then, the concrete walls on either side of the stranger started to turn black.

Dark stains started to spread out along the face of the walls, like patches of water soaking through the concrete, and long, veiny tendrils of black snaked out of the growing central blotches.

And then, though Jack could scarcely believe it, *things* started to emerge from these patches of black. Writhing bodies, coated in slick, red blood, pulled themselves from what should have been a solid wall, groaning and moaning. Though they were of human shape, these deformed things were clearly something else: elongated limbs and small white bulbs lining the flesh, and features that were stretched or twisted, like some kind of horrific abstract painting.

Though Jack was seeing all of this quite clearly in the beam of his flashlight, it was nevertheless slow in registering as reality in his mind, so fantastical was the horrifying sight. He kept thinking that it wasn't real—couldn't be real—and that something embarrassingly obvious would soon reveal itself to be the cause of it all, then the universe would once again fall into a natural order he understood.

But, as the bodies—scores of them now—continued to pull themselves into this reality, realisation and acceptance eventually dawned on him. This was real. As nightmarish and impossible as it seemed, it *was* real. Jack was shaking, both from fear, and from a sudden surge in adrenaline that shot through his body.

Fight or flight mode kicked in. Fighting, he knew, was just not an option, so that left only one alternative. Eventually, Jack found his voice as he turned to flee.

'Run!' he screamed to Andrew. 'Fucking run!'

And so they did, both sprinting down the hallway, back to the machine room from which they had just come. Jack was aware that they were heading deeper into the building, rather than escaping, but what other option did they have? Facing the horrors behind them was an even crazier prospect than staying inside this place.

His heart pounded in his chest, spiked both by shock and terror, and the exertion of running just about as fast as he ever had. Given that Jack was the slimmer, fitter, of the two, he easily pulled ahead of his partner. However, he quickly felt a pang of guilt at letting Andrew fall behind. If those things caught up, it would be the bigger man who took the fall.

Though perhaps that would give Jack further chance to escape?

As scared as he was—and he was terrified—the shame of such a thought caused him to ease up a touch, just as they closed in on the doorway to the machine room. Casting a look back over his shoulder, he was momentarily blinded by the beam from Andrew's torch as the bigger man followed. But, just before the light engulfed his vision and briefly seared his retinas, Jack was sure that he saw multiple figures lumbering after them both, lurching though the dark.

Horrible, low moans echoed down the hallway after them as well, which confirmed that those creatures were giving chase. However, Jack couldn't be sure how quickly they were moving.

They both barrelled through into the machine room, before quickly turning and slamming shut the heavy metal doors. The crash that rang out as the doors smashed against the frame was so loud it momentarily drowned out the approaching wails of the monstrosities outside.

Jack looked at the door he was holding shut, desperate to find some kind of locking mechanism to hold off what followed, but he could see nothing of use. There was a keyhole, but no key. Both he and Andrew then braced themselves, pressing their bodies against the cold metal, ready to try to keep it held shut when the inevitable force from beyond tried to overwhelm them.

But that did not come.

Though he could still hear the moaning from the corridor outside, no force tried to work against them to push the doors open. Panting to catch his breath, Jack looked to Andrew.

'Why aren't they coming through?' he asked, but Andrew just shrugged. Perhaps they were still going to, but were just slower in reaching the end of the corridor than Jack had first assumed. But, after holding their position for close to a minute, with no attempt against them, Jack eventually eased up. He took a knee and tried to angle his torch to send light through the small key-hole. It worked well enough to reveal a mass of red bodies just outside of the door, completely blocking the way. But all were standing motionless, like blood-covered mannequins.

Jack pulled his head back and once again looked to his friend. 'They aren't moving,' he whispered, fearful that raising his voice too much would spur the suddenly—it seemed—docile things outside back into action.

Again, Andrew said nothing. But what was there to say? What insight could he offer? What they had just seen simply should not be possible.

'We can't just stand here like this all night,' Andrew eventually whispered in a breathless voice. 'We need to move.'

He was right of course.

Jack was concerned that if they moved away from the door they were guarding, they would be left exposed, with nothing to stop the nightmares in the corridor from then spilling through. However, it was true that they couldn't stay here indefinitely. And if those things *did* decide to try and force their way through, could the two of them really hope to hold them off anyway? Jack wasn't sure of the exact number of creatures beyond the door, but it was more than enough to overpower the two of them, certainly.

Jack took a breath, then hesitantly backed up—along with Andrew—and the two then made their way further into the room, walking quickly but quietly. As they moved, they passed large industrial control boxes, an old looking furnace, and long unused machines, some of which were guarded by wire cages. Jack kept casting tentative glances back at the door that separated the two police officers from the demonic things outside, expecting them to burst open at any minute. Thankfully, however, that did not happen. But even that caused a knot of unease to form in his gut.

It occurred to him that if those things weren't actually chasing them down to rip them apart, then their aim was suddenly obvious: to stop Jack and Andrew escaping. It was then the words spoken by that hooded figure earlier—*turn back*—made more sense.

Jack and Andrew were being herded.

To where, Jack had no idea. But he knew that if they simply complied like docile cattle, then the outcome for them would surely be terrible.

'We need to figure this out,' Jack said, pulling up to a stop. Andrew halted his march as well, then turned to face Jack, his sweaty brow furrowed in confusion.

'What the hell are you talking about?' he asked. 'Didn't you see what was out there? We need to get away from those things as quickly as we can.'

'But why aren't they following?' Jack asked. 'Something about this isn't right. It doesn't make sense.'

'You got that right!' Andrew exclaimed, throwing his hands up in the air. 'Nothing about this is right. People are coming out of the fucking walls! Nothing is right here, Jack, but we don't need to stick around for it.'

'I get that, but how come they just stopped? I really doubt it's because they couldn't figure out how to work a goddamned door.'

Andrew shook his head and looked as if he were about to argue back, when a sudden sound caught their attention. They quickly turned and looked ahead, towards the noise that was approaching.

Faint at first, and rhythmic, Jack soon recognised the unmistakable *slap, slap, slap* of barefoot running on solid floor. As the footfalls grew louder, and therefore closer, they could hear a heavy breathing and wheezing as well.

Whoever—or whatever—it was that ran towards Jack and Andrew, they sounded like they were really pushing themselves, and panting hard as a result. Jack tensed up and shone his flashlight ahead, towards the door they were heading towards.

Closer and closer.

Considering what Jack had just seen, he had no idea what kind of nightmarish vision would now reveal itself to them. He could sense Andrew tense up beside him and, turning his head, saw that the big man had balled up his fists. Jack tried to control his breathing, to ready himself, and just hoped that, between them, he and his partner had what it took to overcome the thing that approached.

And then it sprinted quickly into the room, before drawing to a sudden stop and bringing its hands up to shield its eyes, surprised by the bright light from the flashlights.

But this thing was no monster. It was a man. Shaven headed and naked, with a look of terror in his eyes.

'Help me,' he pleaded.

'Who are you?' Jack asked of the shivering man, having quickly noticed that—other than being naked—there was something decidedly odd about this person: and that was that strange markings covering much of his skin. Occult-like symbols were cut into the flesh, and ran with blood. One of these markings—an inverted triangle set in two concentric circles—even covered the entirety of the man's chest. Within the triangle, there was an elliptical shape that resembled an eye.

'I've... I've made a mistake,' the man said, frantic. His voice was panicked and his eyes wide. 'I was so wrong. We were *all* so wrong. Help me... please.'

'Tell me what you are doing here,' Jack demanded, trying his best to maintain a calm exterior in the face of such an insane situation. Andrew said nothing, which wasn't normally the case when the two of them confronted a suspect. Granted, they weren't in a normal situation, but that just meant that Andrew was not dealing with this whole thing well.

Fuck, Jack thought. *Am I dealing with this well? Was it even possible to deal with such a situation well?*

Indeed, a naked man with weird carvings in his flesh was perfectly mundane when put up against blood-covered creatures that had crawled out of walls only moments ago.

'Will you help me?' the terrified man pleaded as tears ran down his pale face.

'Yes. Everything will be okay,' Jack said, 'but you need to tell me what you are doing here. What is going on?'

The man shook his head and began to cry. Then he brought his hands up to his face and began to scratch at the skin. 'Stupid,' he said. 'Stupid, stupid, stupid. I was just a pawn. We all were.'

Jack assessed the potential threat from this man and deduced it was likely minimal. The stranger seemed terrified, and was hardly concealing a hidden weapon. Regardless, Jack was experienced enough to know that even the most unassuming people could surprise you. And often in the worst way. He decided that his approach would be to offer help and support, initially. Until, that was, this person gave him reason to consider him dangerous.

The man clearly knew at least *something* of what was going on here, and Jack and Andrew could use any information they might be able to get.

'What's your name?' he asked in a tone that was as gentle and as unconfrontational as he could make it. The man's eyes then rose to meet Jack's and, after a moment, he answered.

'B... Brian.'

'Okay, Brian, what were you running from?'

Brian took a moment to reply to that. When he did, the response was unsettling to say the least.

'Hell.'

Just as Jack was trying to make sense of that reply, the doors behind them all suddenly burst open.

Spinning around, Jack aimed the flashlight to see those blood-covered things come spilling into the machine room, moaning wildly as they did.

'Run!' Andrew screamed, and the two officers sprinted forward, with Jack grabbing hold of Brian in order to pull him along with them.

'No!' he cried, twisting his arm in Jack's grip. 'We can't go back.'

Jack held firm and pulled him along with them. 'We can't stay here,' he ordered.

Brian looked to the approaching hoard and his face dropped. 'We're doomed.'

Ignoring the defeatist—though probably accurate—summation, Jack pulled Brian along with him and Andrew as they ran through the doorway Brian had emerged from only moments before. Jack quickly slammed the heavy door shut behind them as they passed over the threshold, but given there was no lock to keep it permanently shut, they continued sprinting down the new corridor they found themselves in. Swaying and flickering beams from the torches lit the way ahead, showing yet another concrete passageway that was otherwise completely dark. Doors lined the wall on both sides, and Jack had a feeling they led to other rooms, but probably ones with no way out. If they tried one and found themselves trapped within, then it was game over. So, he kept on going.

Eventually, Jack could see that the corridor ahead became a t-junction and split both left and right. So they had a quick decision to make.

Listening intently as they continued to sprint as hard as they could, Jack realised that he could no longer hear the groans and moans from the shambling horde that had been giving chase. He quickly looked back, shining his light, and saw that nothing was giving chase. At least, not quickly.

Had those things stopped again?

Jack once more got the feeling that he and Andrew—and now this mysterious stranger, Brian—were simply being herded, by design, rather than actually being chased. But he did not get a chance to vocalise that as another sound up ahead caused him to jump.

A groan. This one human.

Then a bloody hand came into view from the left-hand side, grabbing on to the corner of the wall. All three men stopped. 'This is madness,' Andrew said, clearly panicked.

'Nothing behind us,' Jack stated, looking back. 'I think they've stopped again.'

A gurgling sound caused all three of them to then focus on that hand, and what was now crawling into view.

It was another man, and—like Brian—he was also naked. His shoulders and upper torso emerged from around the corner as he pulled himself along, chest sliding across the floor as he moved.

The man's face was etched with horror and agony, and blood bubbled from his mouth. But he kept pulling himself forward, revealing more of him to the trio, and also revealing the reason for his obvious pain. Jack saw that the man's body simply ended at his midsection. The flesh there was torn and ripped, as if his body had been violently ripped in two, and a stringy, mushy mesh of glistening red meat slopped out to the floor behind. The man didn't make it far before a long death rattle wheezed from his lips, and his head dropped to the ground, eyes glassy. His body became motionless. Intestines sprawled from the end of his torso like crimson ropes, and they partially covered a severed spine. Whatever had happened to this poor stranger, it must have occurred only moments ago. There was simply no way he could have survived for long in that condition.

Which meant that something very dangerous lay around the corner to the left.

'What the fuck is going on here, Brian?' Jack demanded.

No sooner had he spoken than he heard a wet shuffling sound. Turning the beam of his torch behind them, Jack could just make out the blood-covered monstrosities shuffling down the corridor again, through the darkness, though their desperate moans had now ceased. 'Fuck!' he seethed through gritted teeth, and ran forward again, Andrew following. These things had snuck up on them, moving silently through the darkness.

Jack again pulled Brian with him, seeing that the strange man could not take his eyes off the mutilated body that they passed as they moved to the right.

Jack didn't dare cast his eyes back again as they moved, instead concentrating straight ahead, sprinting farther down the corridor. A loud and horrible skittering sound emanated out from the darkness behind—the same direction from which the dead man had just crawled. A sudden screeching then ripped through the air—sounds that were monstrous and alien.

'Save me, please!' Brian screamed, still being pulled along. 'Please. We need to get out of here. We'll all die. We need to get out. Please, help me. Please!'

Brian was becoming hysterical, but he was begging for salvation that Jack couldn't offer. The chances of any of them making it out alive suddenly seemed very unlikely. A weird night had suddenly transformed into something unbelievable and horrifying, and he sensed it was likely to only get worse.

On top of that, Jack wasn't even sure that Brian could be trusted. It was clear that the naked man who ran alongside with them was somehow involved in all of this. How could he not be, considering the condition he was in and all of those strange markings on his body? And what was it he had said?

I was so wrong. We were all *so wrong.*

'We need to find a different path,' Brian begged. 'We can't go back this way.'

But Jack didn't listen. Couldn't listen. There wasn't time —too much madness behind, bearing down on them.

The three men then turned another corner and, up ahead, Jack saw a dull light. The corridor seemed to end with an open doorway, through which a flickering glow spilled through.

'No,' Brian pleaded. More loud screeching from behind, and a vile chattering too: insect-like, but impossibly loud. Just how big was the unseen creature that made such a sound?

Big enough to rip a man in two, Jack thought to himself. They had seen the savage result of that only moments ago.

With no other choice, the group pushed on, sprinting out of the corridor and through the open doorway.

Right into Hell.

They were now in the guts of the facility, Jack knew. That much was clear to him as he looked about the vast space.

Whatever the purpose this building had served, the place they now stood had clearly been the heart of the operation. Other corridors and rooms—some of which they had recently come through—were all periphery. Useful appendages, or arteries that ran off and existed to service this central heart.

The circular room—such as it was—that they now stood in was huge. The low ceilings of the passageways were now gone, and the area around them rose up—and up—ending in darkness that swallowed up everything from about the fifty-foot mark. For Jack, it was like being inside the stomach of a huge rocket, looking up at a hollow internal structure, but the circumference of this place was much wider.

There wasn't much machinery here to speak of, but it was easy to tell where equipment had once stood. Lighter coloured patches on the concrete floor littered the ground and showed the outlines of where equipment once stood. Pipework high up above them branched out from the walls and then stopped, having obviously been cut off some time ago. It was clear that this place had been stripped out of anything remotely valuable or useful, unlike the machine room they had been in earlier. Metal gangways ran at different levels above them as well, crisscrossing from the circular outer walls, where steel stairwells also rose. And the light in the room was afforded by scores of candles that had been set about the floor, gangways, and stairwells, all casting off a yellow, flickering light that managed to puncture much of the darkness at this low level.

But those were all mundane details. Things that Jack's mind registered as normal. Or close to normal. Perhaps they could have been of vague interest to him, were it not for the fact that the whole area had been desecrated with... well, Jack couldn't determine exactly what, exactly.

As soon as he had entered this space, his terrified gaze had immediately been drawn to the gigantic, writhing thing that stood central in the area, towering up to an unknown height as it disappeared into the darkness above. Roughly cylindrical, it was enough to almost give Jack a heart attack. The flesh of this seemingly living tower was a deep, glistening red, with tumour-like growths along its surface—clusters of different sized lumps, some tiny, others bigger than Jack himself. Then there were the eyes—thousands of the white, fleshy orbs with rolling black spots in their centre. There were pulsating areas of flesh, too, like small bubbles forming on the surface of a vast lake.

But there was more.

Much of the vast, circular, outer wall of the room was also covered in a pulsating, flesh-like webbing, that seemed to tendril out from the monstrosity at the centre. And more of those blood-covered creatures that had been hunting the group roamed this area, and there were dozens of naked men—like Brian—held prisoner by the demon-like things, and these men were screaming for mercy. These men also had occult-like symbols cut into their skin. They were fighting for their lives, but overpowered by the strength of the inhuman things that restrained them. And, one by one, these poor people were being led towards the towering, central mass.

If that wasn't enough, there were others present in the room as well. Robed figures, who stood completely still, simply observing what was happening around them, but left completely alone by the demons that restrained the prisoners.

Some were clad in dark red, others a dull blue. Looking up, Jack also noticed another figure that stood on one of the gangways, elevated from the rest. This person was dressed in black, a hood covering his face, like the others. He was clearly someone of importance, given his position, as he looked down, watching over proceedings. Jack had a feeling that man was the same person who had earlier ordered them to turn back.

All of these details hit Jack immediately as he, and the other two, sprinted into this large space, but the scene overwhelmed him. Especially that... *thing*... in the middle of it all. It took Jack a moment to remember that they were actually being chased and, as the hooded strangers slowly turned to face him, Jack quickly spun and looked back. Yet again shining his light to pierce the dark, he saw the horde were standing motionless, packed into the narrow hallway outside, blocking any escape, but no longer advancing. He had a feeling that they had succeeded in shepherding Jack and Andrew where they had always intended to.

Jack saw something else, beyond the horde—something that emitted the same screeching that he had earlier heard as they ran. The thing was huge, standing tall behind the smaller humanoid creatures in front of it. To call it a demon would have been accurate, but it was more than that: a massive, multi-legged thing. It filled the space of the corridor, illuminated by the shaking of Jack's torchlight. White, wispy hairs covered the lumpy body of this creature, its powerful appendages all spread out, pressing against the walls and ceiling round it, holding it in place. Smaller twitching arms dangled from a bald underbelly that sat upright, and the face of the monster was alien—a mass of eyes and a vertical mouth that slowly opened and closed, chewing on the lower half of a torso. Jack could see a single leg dangle from the disgusting maw. The thing was an insectoid nightmare.

And the realisation that it had been crawling around this place with them was terrifying. What other horrors were lurking in this facility?

But Jack could not afford to worry about that now, as his attention was turned back to the main area around him.

Someone had spoken.

It was a single word, shouted from up above, and it echoed through the air, loud enough to be heard over the frantic screaming of those that were held against their will.

It came from the black-robed person up on the gantry. The male voice was hoarse and rasping.

'*Welcome.*'

'What the hell is going on?' Andrew demanded loudly, suddenly finding his voice.

Part of Jack wanted answers as well—for the sake of his own sanity, if nothing else—but he had a feeling that any explanation to this madness would not really help matters, only make things worse. It took Jack a few moments to realise that Andrew was not vocalising the question towards him. Rather, to those in the room.

Andrew stepped forward, marching closer to some of those demons, who were now watching him with interest, but their proximity did not seem deter him. Jack considered that Andrew had lost his damn mind.

'Andrew!' Jack snapped. 'What the fuck are you doing? Get back here.'

Andrew didn't pay any attention. Brian had dropped down on the floor beside Jack and was sobbing, clearly defeated. He kept whispering the same word over and over again as he hugged himself and rocked. 'No, no, no, no.'

Andrew eventually stopped his purposeful strides, now standing in amongst all of the scattered prisoners, robed figures, and monstrous creatures that inhabited the space. And he did not seem to fear attack, though he did keep a respectful distance from the towering, pulsating mass in the centre of the room. Andrew cast his eyes up to the figure high above them on the gantry.

The watcher in black.

'I could have been killed!' Andrew yelled. 'You started too early. I demand answers!'

Jack's mind was swimming. His partner and friend was talking like he knew that stranger high above them. *What the fuck is going on?*

The man in black then responded in his distorted, unnatural voice. It was loud... and angry. '*You do not demand anything of us, you mewling wretch.*'

Andrew immediately took a step back, almost cowering, seemingly fearful of angering whoever the man was.

'I'm... I'm sorry, Mr. Ainsworth,' Andrew said, holding up his hands in supplication. 'I just... I wasn't expecting things to have started already. I brought the sacrifice, as we agreed.' Andrew was pointing at Jack now, who suddenly felt nauseous. The realisation of betrayal started to wash over him. Andrew went on, 'But I could have died.'

'*You were guided here,*' the man above said. Mr. Ainsworth, apparently. '*As we willed it.*'

Brian was still muttering to himself on the floor next to Jack. Still rocking. And scratching at his skin.

'What the fuck is going on?' Jack whispered down to him, desperate for answers. He then knelt down beside the naked man and grabbed him by the shoulders, shaking him hard. 'Talk to me, damn it!'

'*You need not ask that lowly creature,*' the robed man in the gantry answered, now addressing Jack. '*Your... partner... can answer all of your questions.*'

Jack turned to Andrew, who was now looking back at him. 'What the fuck have you done?'

'Don't you presume to judge me,' Andrew said through gritted teeth. There was determination in the larger man's eyes, and a wild expression that Jack had never seen before. 'You don't know anything.'

'You... you brought me here on purpose?' Jack asked, rage bubbling in his voice. 'For this?'

'I did,' Andrew stated, jutting out his jaw defiantly.

'Why?'

'Because I was told to. Because there are bigger things than us in this life. Things that must be obeyed. So, I fulfil my role and bring souls here when needed.'

Jack managed to repress a sudden urge to dash forward, wrap his hands around Andrew's neck, and squeeze for all he was worth. But, given the odds he faced—not least of all Andrew himself, who was more than capable of swatting Jack away like a fly—Jack forced himself to hold off. All he could do now, he knew, was to buy for time and see if an opportunity to escape presented itself. Hopefully that would happen before these maniacs followed through with whatever they were planning for him.

'So, you're a servant?' Jack asked, taunting his partner. 'A little delivery boy for these nutcases.'

Andrew stepped forward towards Jack. 'I'm part of something bigger. Soon, you will be, too.' A cruel smirk formed over his lips. 'Though, in a different way altogether.'

'And these?' Jack asked, motioning to the naked prisoners. 'Who are they?'

'*Fools*,' the man above—Ainsworth—answered. '*Puppets who thought they would join our ranks. Filled with false promises and glimpses of things greater than they are. But they are little more than food. Fodder. Sustenance. A necessary part of the ritual to summon the Great Ashklaar.'* Ainsworth pointed a bony finger at the sickening, fleshy tower in the centre of the room.

At the mention of its name, a completely alien and terrifying sound boomed from the strange form—a distorted hum unlike anything Jack could have ever imagined. It disoriented him instantly, bored into his mind, and caused him to cry out in pain. He even vomited remnants of his lunch to the floor, the bile spilling down onto his boots, such was the dizzying effect of the nightmarish sound.

The prisoners in the room all had a similar reaction as well. Some rolled around on the floor, pressing their hands to their ears, while others started sobbing loudly. Most, however, screamed for mercy.

Through teary eyes, Jack saw that most of the robed figures present had all taken a knee, including Ainsworth, as if supplicating to royalty. But they didn't seem to be in any pain. Eventually, the horrible sounds faded, and Jack was again able to get his bearings.

Ainsworth looked down at them all. *'More!'* he ordered.

A screech went up from the blood-covered demons, and a group of naked men were dragged screaming towards the pulsating tower of flesh. Jack counted seven in total.

'Noooooooooo,' the leading man screamed in terror, his voice hitting a pitch higher than Jack had ever heard from a man. The petrified prisoner fought against his captors, but it was useless, as he was utterly overpowered. The blood-covered demons dragged him forward, and others behind him, towards the living tower. 'I beg you,' he cried.

But his pleas were ignored. Jack then bore witness to the feeding of Ashklaar.

Had Jack not already just emptied his stomach, then he would have surely done so after witnessing this sickening sacrifice. Though, an empty stomach didn't stop him from wretching continuously at the display.

The chosen victims were forced close to the surface of the twitching mass, and the hundreds of bulbous eyes that lined the fleshy pillar began to flit about in a frenzy, as if excited by what was coming.

Jack could see no obvious way for the thing to take the sacrifices, with no arms or mouth to speak of.

But then he saw it.

The first prisoner was pushed farther forward, and his naked skin pressed into the foul, undulating surface of the immense, living pillar. He started to scream. An agonising cry that cut to Jack's core, causing his blood to run cold, such was the obvious and instant agony this poor man was in.

The flesh of the unknown entity then seemed to expand and the tumorous form puckered around the form of its victim. The man's screaming was cut off as his face was covered by the encroaching mass. Jack saw blood spill from the twitching prisoner, running down the space where the engorging flesh sucked at him. Steam rose from the contact, as well as a smell so foul that it caused Jack to dry-heave.

Jack recognised this odour, having experienced it once before when he had rushed inside of a burning house to help the people inside. He had been too late, of course, and the fire had been so severe that the old couple inside had practically melted to their beds. The memories of that smell were triggered now, as it was identical to that coming from the suffering man, whose flesh was quite clearly melting from the touch of that terrible pillar.

The slow engulfing continued, and Jack could see that some areas of the demonic flesh had opened up, sucking the gooey mess of the victim inside. Eventually, the poor man vanished completely within the mass that closed up behind him. It twitched and pulsated, excitedly.

Jack then realised that this horrific end was to be his fate, too. Andrew had tricked him and lured him here for this very purpose. What else could it be?

'*Another!*' Ainsworth ordered, and the sickening show started again with another victim. The man screamed and resisted, just as the last had done, but history repeated itself. The searing touch as he was engulfed by the tumorous flesh. The smell... Oh God, the smell.

Jack looked around, panicked, desperately seeking a way out. Many doors lined the perimeter of the circular space, all closed, but each could either lead to escape, or right into the path of more horrendous creatures. If he even got that far. The odds of him evading capture and actually reaching one of these doors were not good.

But if he didn't try, he knew what was waiting for him. What was it that the man above had called it? Ashklaar?

As it turned out, Brian was thinking of escape as well,

and after the second feeding, he suddenly leapt to his feet and ran, off to his left, sprinting as fast as he could and screeching in absolute fear.

He did not get far.

The same demons Jack had earlier seen crawling from the walls quickly descended on him, moving at a speed Jack had not previously seen. Impossibly fast, they moved with an ape-like gait, pushing along on their long arms. As they moved, they would disappear for a moment, suddenly appearing a few yards ahead, phasing in and out of reality. A group of four quickly and effortlessly caught up with Brian and easily forced him to the ground.

Lying on his back, Brian screamed and wailed as each of the monsters took a limb, holding him on the floor. They then turned their nightmarish and twisted faces up to Ainsworth, seemingly awaiting instruction from him.

Jack new that Brian would be the next sacrifice to the monstrous pillar that these robed figures seemed to worship.

But that was not what happened.

'He is yours,' Ainsworth said. 'Indulge!'

And they did.

As other men were fed to Ashklaar, those creatures that held Brian tore him apart as he shrieked in agony. And they did it slowly, taking great pleasure in pain as limbs were ripped from his torso. And Jack could see it all from his position.

First, the right leg was twisted and pulled free, like a cooked chicken leg, with surprising ease. Blood gushed from the bloody and fleshy stump at the hip that had now became exposed. Stringy veins held the detached limb to the main body for a moment, and were quickly snapped, spitting out more crimson blood. Next came the arms, followed by his last leg. The man continued to scream himself hoarse as he bled out in an ever-increasing pool of his own blood. Helpless, like a squirming fly stripped of its legs and wings.

But, even after suffering unbelievable pain and torture, and knowing he was going to die, there was more yet for Brian to endure. One of the creatures gripped his head, under his chin, as another took hold of the torso at the shoulders. He was then hoisted up, held between the two monsters... and they pulled, making an excited sound akin to cackling as they did. Brian's screams renewed. His neck actually seemed to stretch a little at first, but then the skin began to split. More blood poured from the widening wound that first appeared at his throat, then ran around to the back of his neck. Vibrating vocal chords were revealed as the head was pulled further away. Brian's jaw still moved as the chords ripped apart completely just as they hit an almost impossibly high pitch, ceasing completely mid-scream. The head then fully detached, and Brian was finally allowed the mercy of death.

But the monsters were not finished with his body. After acting out the cruel and prolonged torture, the four creatures then started to devour his flesh, pulling open the stomach and feasting on intestines that were pulled free. It shouldn't have been possible, but what remained of the man's body was stripped down to bone within minutes.

Thoughts of escape quickly fell away as Jack realised there was no way out. He could do nothing to save himself. So he instead fell to the ground, collapsing to a sitting position, and started to cry. Through teary eyes he looked back over to Andrew, whose pleased sneer now showed the real man, and not the false veneer that had deceived Jack for the past year.

Then a realisation hit.

The past year.

Trevor—Andrew's former partner—had died here a year ago. And now Jack suddenly realised what had happened to him.

'You killed Trevor, too?' Jack confirmed out loud.

Andrew shrugged. 'Not directly. But I brought him here as a sacrifice. To prove myself.'

'You fucker!' Jack seethed.

If Jack was going to die, then he at least wanted to try and take this back-stabbing piece of shit with him. He doubted he could take the larger man in a straight fight, but the thought of rushing Andrew and trying to rip his throat clean open was still a welcome one. And it would at least be a last act of defiance before his life was taken from him in some horrific manner.

But Jack never got the chance.

'*Seize him!*' Ainsworth ordered from above, and the dutiful creatures pounced. Jack braced himself.

But it was not him they took hold of.

It was Andrew.

'What are you doing?' Andrew yelled, clearly as surprised at this development as Jack was.

Andrew was quickly overpowered, as the previous victims had been, and his clothing was then torn from his body, leaving him completely naked. Finally, he was pushed to his knees as he struggled uselessly and shouted out in anger.

One of the creatures took his head in its large hands and forced him to look up at the mysterious Ainsworth above—he who seemed to hold command over everyone here.

Well, all apart from one.

It was quite clear that Ainsworth, too, served the thing which had just received the sacrifices. That terrible, unknowable monster, which Jack was forced to consider. Did that thing reside here permanently? If that was the case, and foul demons did indeed lurk in this building—then surely someone would have encountered and reported them before now. If they had survived, of course.

So, if they weren't here permanently, then where had they come from? Jack suspected the answer was relatively simple, if completely bat-shit crazy. Ainsworth had spoken of a ritual to summon Ashklaar. And here it was, in all its eldritch glory. These other creatures, Jack reasoned, had been summoned along with it.

'*We thank you for your loyalty, Andrew,*' Ainsworth boomed from above.

Jack was now certain this was the same figure that they had seen on the video camera earlier, and the same person who had commanded them to turn back while in the corridor. But given the way the man spoke—the horrible, distorted sound of his voice—Jack wasn't certain he was actually human. At least, not entirely.

'What the fuck are you talking about?' Andrew seethed. 'I've done everything you've asked of me!'

'*You have. But not without issue. The one you brought last year resulted in a lot of loose ends. You were sloppy. So, now there is a choice to be made as to whether or not you carry on in your current position. Or if you become one with the Old God as he feasts on your body and soul.*'

'I'll carry on,' Andrew pleaded, his voice laced with both panic and terror. 'And I'll do a better job. I swear.'

A sinister chuckle came from Ainsworth. '*You will not decide this.*' His arm straightened and a long finger protruded from the dark, baggy cloth, pointing straight at Jack. '*He will.*'

Those words didn't sink in straight away for Jack. *He* would decide Andrew's fate?

'What?' Andrew was incredulous, and obviously still just as confused as Jack. 'Him? Why? This is insane. He is a sacrifice. One I brought for you, just as you asked.'

'*He is someone we have been watching for a long time,*' Ainsworth corrected. '*Meticulous in what he does. Considered* in his actions. *Calm under pressure. The perfect qualities we require in your... replacement.'*

'No! This can't be happening. I've been loyal. I've done everything asked. You can't betray me like this. You can't!'

'*Silence!*' Ainsworth thundered, angrily. The power of his voice was like a sonic explosion, loud enough that both Andrew and Jack jumped back, startled. '*You will say no more, only await your fate. If you utter one more word, you will not even have the pleasure and honour of being a sacrifice.*' After hearing this, the blood-covered demons started baying with excitement. Jack could tell Andrew wanted to argue. His desperation to make his master see sense was written all over his face. But Andrew restrained himself, clearly knowing that the leader presiding over this madness would carry through with this threat.

So, instead, Andrew turned to Jack, and the look of desperate pleading on his face was both pathetic and amusing.

At least to Jack.

He'd never thought of himself as a vengeful man before, but quickly realised he'd never truly been in a position where vengeance was warranted. Now he was, though, and the thought of it, of getting payback on a man he'd considered—only minutes ago—a true friend, was an enticing one.

The idea of becoming a replacement, however—of luring people to their death—was not something Jack wanted to be any part of. He was well aware of the kind of choice on offer here, even before Ainsworth went on to put it into words, turning his attention to Jack.

'*Jack Collings. You have a choice to make of the utmost importance. And it is not one that you should make lightly. What is it to be, this man's life or your own? But, be warned, if you choose to spare your own existence, then it belongs to us. You will live to serve us above all others and obey our every command. If you fail at this, we will take you and all those you hold dear, and your souls shall know only eternal torment. However, if you decide against taking your place as our servant, then Mr. Andrew Todd here has a second chance. And you will take his place as the sacrifice. So, Mr. Collings, what will it be? Will you join us?'*

Jack looked around at all of those who were gathered: robed cultists and vile abominations alike. Even at the towering nightmare that they all worshiped. Then, he turned to Andrew again. Tears were now streaming down his face, but he was still under orders not to speak. The pitiful pleading expression he wore was instead his way of begging Jack for mercy.

But was there really a decision to be made at all? Even if Andrew was worth saving, then it would mean Jack's own life was forfeit. And as it was, Andrew had proven himself to be beyond contempt. A selfish parasite who was willing to let others die in a horrific manner simply to save himself and worship this fucking eldritch nightmare. That man deserved nothing less than what was coming to him.

'I'll join you,' Jack said as his head hung low. The instant he uttered those words, Andrew started to scream manically and thrash against the things that held him.

'No! No! No!'

But it was futile, and he was dragged towards the thing that Ainsworth had called Ashklaar.

A sinking feeling gnawed its way through Jack's gut. Though he had managed to save himself, he was well aware that his life going forward was going to be vastly different. He was, in effect, going to become exactly what Andrew had been. So was he really any better than his soon-to-be ex-partner? Should he really judge so quickly? And, if

Ainsworth and his followers had been so quick to discard Andrew, how long could Jack really hope to last?

It didn't take long for the demons to drag Andrew towards the awaiting, pulsating pillar. A thundering and dizzying sound boomed out from it, causing all around to cower. Jack toppled to a knee, but managed to maintain just enough balance not to fall flat on his face. The sound faded, but Andrew's desperate screams continued.

'Please, Jack, you can't do this. Don't let it happen. Please. I'm begging you. You can't let them do this to me. Please!'

Andrew was close to the surface of Ashklaar now, held only inches away. Unlike the first victim Jack had seen fed to this thing, Andrew was made to face away from it. If there was a significance to this, it was lost on Jack.

At first.

But then Ainsworth spoke again. '*Prove yourself,*' he said to Jack in that unnaturally loud voice, booming down from his position on the gantry. '*If we are to trust you, then it falls to you to sacrifice your friend. A simple push, ending his life in this existence, and damning his soul forever to the will of the ancient Ashhklaar. Only then will we accept you.*'

Jack took a breath. Condemning Andrew to that horrific fate was one thing, but actually being the one to physically send him into oblivion? That was something else entirely. And Jack wasn't sure he was capable of such a thing. Andrew continued to beg as Jack wrestled with his conscience.

'*Well?*' Ainsworth asked.

Another breath, this time to steady himself. Then Jack walked forward.

His mind made up.

'Jack, please,' Andrew sobbed as Jack stepped up to him. 'You can't. I beg you. It isn't just death. The torture will never end.'

A small part of Jack did actually feel sorry for Andrew, and he hated himself for what he was about to do. But he knew he was justified in his actions and vocalised that to his former friend. 'Sorry, Andrew. But you were perfectly happy to let this happen to me. So, enjoy your never-ending torture.'

The demons that held Andrew seemed pleased and emitted excited chunters. This was as close as Jack had been to them since this whole thing began, and at this distance he could make out more details under the coating of blood: the small white blobs that lined the skin—alien eyes with dark pupils at the centre—all constantly moved in different directions, just as they did on the massive form of Ashklaar. The flesh, covered by blood, was lined with creases that resembled muscle and sinew, as if skin that had once been there had since been ripped off. No two faces of these things were alike. Some were a little more human than others, but most were distinctly demonic. All, however, were twisted, deformed, and terrifying.

And the monsters were also quite clearly deadly.

'Please,' Andrew begged again, but he had closed his eyes now, and his voice sounded defeated. As much as the man obviously didn't want it to happen, he seemed to be resigned to his fate.

'I'm sorry,' Jack said, partially meaning it. Then he thrust his hands forward, pushing Andrew back as hard as he could. In that same instant, the demons that held Andrew released him and, though Andrew was much bigger than Jack, Jack was able to exert sufficient force to make Andrew stumble a step.

And that was all it took.

The instant his skin made contact with the flesh of the Old God, Andrew screamed. Jack could make out a thick liquid secreting out from the meat of the living pillar, adhering to Andrew's skin. And that same liquid began to sear and burn. Like a fly caught in a web, Andrew was held perfectly still as the body of Ashklaar began to slowly envelop and devour him, melting his flesh and pulling him further into its form as a void slowly opened up around Andrew's body, just enough to slowly suck him inside and let the thick, destructive liquid melt through his skin. His flesh started to boil and split as it was stripped away.

Andrew's cries of anguish, coupled with the smell of cooking meat, were more than Jack could bear, but he sensed that his role here was to keep watching. After all, the gazes of those robed figures were not trained on the disgusting sacrifice that was taking place, but rather on him, on Jack, gauging his reaction. So, Jack continued to observe the horrific scene before him.

Andrew continued to be slowly pulled inside of the vile

mass—unable to move, only to feel. The disgusting ooze, that burned like acid and continued to mercilessly eat away at him, had now coated Andrew's entire face, melting away the skin to reveal a grinning skull behind. The heat was so fierce that Andrew's eyeballs burst and spat clear liquid from the sockets. Jack felt a violent urge to gag again, but fought against it, somehow managing to keep himself relatively composed.

Eventually, however, Jack was given respite, as his ex-partner—still twitching and squirming—eventually disappeared completely within the mass that closed around him.

The gruesome hissing of melting flesh and spattering of blood were finally muffled, and the room then grew unnervingly quiet. Jack felt faint, and his shaking legs threatened to give out. He held on, fighting to keep upright, waiting for whatever was going to happen next to unfold.

And he waited.

But no one spoke. Then, he realised why. At first he thought it could have been some kind of optical illusion caused by the flickering of the candles, but Jack was soon sure this was no trick of the eye: the thing that had just devoured Andrew had begun to fade away.

The robed figures all looked to the walkway above—up to Ainsworth—and Jack did the same, following their gaze. He saw that Ainsworth was making his way to the steps at the end of the gantry. He was moving at a painfully slow pace, clearly not in any rush.

Jack's anxiety grew.

After all he had experienced tonight, his heart rate still continued to climb, to the point he thought he could well suffer a heart attack. Jack knew absolutely nothing about the people he was dealing with here—if they even *were* people—except that they were able to summon and communicate with some hideous, eldritch god. And he was unsure, at best, if they would be the type of people to honour any kind of deal that they had struck. Perhaps they still planned to feed him to their God—something, Jack guessed, that could never really be sated.

Eventually, the hidden figure in the black robe reached Jack and stood directly before him, taller than he'd seemed at first from such a distance. After a moment's pause, Ainsworth—who loomed over Jack—reached up and pulled back his hood and for the first time revealed his hideous and ancient face.

Pale skin was blotched with sores, welts, and blisters, and dotted with liverspots. It was pulled tightly over a skeletal face, and Jack could see deep purple veins criss-crossing beneath the surface. His scalp was barely covered by thin, wispy white hair, and his nose had a pronounced and distinctive hook to it. The teeth behind thin, black lips were yellowed and cracked. Blood continued to run from his nostrils and from his eye sockets, where the eyes themselves were as black as tar, with no discernible pupils or sclera. Only obsidian orbs.

Eventually, Ainsworth spoke.

'*Very good,*' the ancient-looking man said, his voice still unnatural... almost demonic, his breath as foul as sewerage. '*You are ours now, Mr. Collings. We own you. Now and forever. But how long you get to keep your life and soul remains to be seen. Disappoint us, and... well, you have seen what happened to Mr. Todd.*' Ainsworth sneered and went on. '*We will impart any knowledge you require in good time, but I imagine you have questions?*'

Jack had thousands, and they were all swirling around his mind like a whirlwind. And yet he struggled to reach up and pluck out a single one.

'Why did you need me?' he eventually asked. 'I mean, you fed a lot of people to that... thing,' and he pointed to the tall, fading pillar that reached up and disappeared into darkness above. 'Why did you even need me? Surely you had enough poor souls already?'

Ainsworth seemed to consider the question for a moment. '*The annual summoning of the Great God required a precise ritual. Every year we are able to pull Ashklaar into our reality, at least in small part. And every year its power here grows stronger. So, we continue on our path of servitude. And while we are able to bring many a follower into our number, like lambs to the slaughter, we also require an untarnished soul as well.'*

'Untarnished? What the hell does that mean?'

'The markings you have seen on the chosen ones, they are part of the ritual. Used to bring Ashklaar and his minions into existence here. But those that are marked, though needed to start the ritual, are also therefore tarnished, their souls soured by the language of this Great Old God. And for it to truly gain something from this cycle, to help it strengthen its link to our world, a final sacrifice is needed. A pure soul.'

'I highly doubt Andrew Todd was pure,' Jack said.

Ainsworth chuckled. *'No, I don't suppose you would think that. But he was not marked. His soul was therefore fresh to the Old One. And now, the ritual is finished. Successful. And one year from now, we will honour Ashklaar again, and his connection will grow stronger still, until he is ready to truly enter our realm and claim dominance over all.'*

Jack looked again to the terrible god that Ainsworth spoke of. Its presence here had almost faded away completely, phased out of reality—or at least, Jack's reality—and the shadows and room behind were now clearly visible through its transparent form. Eventually, it—along with the blood covered minions—faded out completely, leaving nothing behind as evidence that such a thing ever existed in the first place.

'And if I don't want that to happen?' Jack asked. 'I mean, it sounds like it would be hell on earth.'

'Oh, it would be much worse,' Ainsworth replied with a smirk. *'To the unchosen, that is. But it is inevitable. It will happen with or without your help. Having a police officer under our control is advantageous, but our plans do not rest on your*

cooperation, make no mistake about that. And we know every-thing about you, Jack. We know about everyone you care for and we know where each and every one of those people lives. Your poor old parents, for example. How would they cope if we were to take them? Can you imagine the horrors we would inflict upon them? Then, one by one, we would work our way through everyone you cared about, and there would be no way for you to find or stop us. Only then, after we have broken you completely, would we take you. So, am I to think you mean to cause us a problem, Mr. Collings?'

Jack stayed quiet at first, letting the threat—one he truly believed they would carry out—sink in.

Did he really have a choice? Agreeing to come out here tonight to help Andrew had set something in motion that he was powerless to stop.

His only chance—and the only chance for his family—was to go along with what was asked of him. If he was lucky, this insidious cult and its apocalyptic plan would be derailed by someone—or something—else in the future, before they could see it through. And if not, perhaps he would be able to prove himself to this cult and spare himself and his family should this apocalypse come to pass.

It was a fantastical and absolutely insane decision to have to make, and even worse, he had to make it straight away. Ultimately, however, it all came down to self-preserva-tion. As it likely had, he realised, with Andrew.

Jack was no better than him, he now knew—he'd simply taken Andrew's place. But he had to make peace with that—and quickly—if he hoped to survive.

'No, sir,' Jack eventually said, bowing his head respect-fully. 'I won't let you down.'

A wide and cruel smile spread across the thin, cracked

lips of Ainsworth. 'Good. Now leave this place. We will contact you when we need you. Be ready.'

The gathered figures then followed Ainsworth as he left the large room through the door from which Jack had entered, leaving him alone inside. He stood in silence—completely motionless—until the last candle went out and darkness consumed him.

He felt terrified. Useless. A pathetic creature and less than a man. Jack had put his own well-being above others. Hell, above the rest of the world, if the insane Ainsworth was to be believed.

And yet, he knew he did not have the bravery to fight against such a thing. So he waited, and formulated an excuse about what had happened to his partner. Jack knew that he couldn't have any of this come back on Ainsworth and the others. After all, they were his masters now.

And he did not want to disappoint them.

THE BOX

3

My name is Michael Telford, and I found that fucking box three weeks ago.

It was a random find, or so I thought at the time. Now, well, now I'm not so sure. I've never been one to hold much stock in fate, but that particular find—for want of a better word—seems to have a purpose.

That box was *meant* for me.

I found it whilst browsing in a charity shop in London that I had not been aware of before. It was tucked away in a side alley, and I stumbled upon it purely by chance while looking for a short-cut. And, to make things even more strange, I usually don't go into charity or secondhand shops, anyway. Tracey, my fiancée, does—she loves them. I've tried to convince myself that I was enticed inside with the idea of getting her a gift—a little trinket to bring a smile to her face.

But I'm not so sure about that.

While looking through the ornaments, baubles, and knick-knacks, I saw it, sat on a shelf, directly in my eyeline and looking totally out of place. Most of the items in the shop looked, dare I say, tacky. This box, though, with its odd carvings and markings, was both intriguing and disturbing in equal measure. Made from a dark redwood and about the size of your average jewellery box, it was surprisingly heavy when I lifted it from the shelf.

I ran my finger along the markings that had been carved into the wood with remarkable skill and clarity. It was hard not to appreciate the craftsmanship, though the symbols and markings could have easily been the work of a madman. They were varied in detail and design, from stick-men-like figures, like those you would see when archaeologists uncover a cave with ancient drawings on them, to more detailed etchings of faces with expressions of horror and pain. The stick figures all seemed to be in the middle of some kind of ritual: either gathered round what appeared to be a fire where one unlucky soul was consumed in flames, or gathered around a dismembered body.

In addition, there was a recurring figure in many of the depictions. A taller, hunched figure who watched the madness from a distance. No matter how detailed the various portrayals were, he was never shown with a face.

Most macabre.

I tried to prise it open, but the lid would not budge, its contents guarded by a lock: three silver scrolling cogs, similar to the number-locks found on briefcases—but with symbols as opposed to numbers. Symbols I had never seen before.

I debated setting the box back on the shelf and moving on, but could not. Why, I do not know. But I wanted it. The strange item didn't have a price tag like the other pieces in the store, so I took it to the till where a small, frail-looking old woman with a blue rinse smiled politely at me. Behind her thin, chapped lips, her teeth had yellowed somewhat.

'Excuse me, how much for this?' I asked, placing the box

into her bony hands. As I did, I felt a pang of regret and urgency, like she would take the box away and say it wasn't for sale.

'My,' she said, confused. 'I'm not sure what this is. Can't rightly say I've seen it before. Very strange.'

'It is,' I agreed. 'But it has a certain charm to it. Is it for sale?'

'Well, I would think so.'

'How much?' I asked, and realised I'd been a bit too eager. Another smile, this one more devious, spread across her lips.

'It's a nice item, good quality. I would imagine, fifty pounds.'

I balked. 'Nonsense. Fifty pounds for an old grubby jewellery box? I won't pay it.'

'Fair enough,' the old woman said with a shrug. And, instead of commencing a haggle as I had suspected she might, the woman simply set it down beneath her desk, out of my view. She gave a smile, which was almost smug.

I wanted the box—though I couldn't explain why—and she could sense that. The crafty old woman, who looked so fragile and easy to manipulate, was obviously someone I'd underestimated.

'Fine,' I said, and handed her the cash. 'But this is daylight robbery.'

'All for a good cause,' she replied. I noticed that she didn't ring the sale up or put the money into the till. She just clutched it tightly in her knobbly fist.

'And what is the cause? I didn't see the sign when I came in. Is it Red Cross, Heart Foundation, or something?'

'No, it's a religious charity, for Christianity,' she replied, and began to cough. The woman patted her chest and regained her composure. 'Smokers cough,' she stated before putting the box into a plastic bag for me.

'Do I get a receipt?' I asked, taking it from her.

'Machine isn't working,' was the answer, though I didn't believe her. 'Enjoy your purchase.'

'Thanks,' I replied. I wasn't really thankful that I'd been conned out of so much money, but I was happy with what I'd received. I left the shop and was halfway down the street when I realised I didn't have anything for Tracey.

~

Over the course of the next two weeks, I tried—in vain—to solve the combination lock and open the damn box. My first few attempts at the lock were complete guesses, and I couldn't tell you know what sequences I tried. After a few failures, I decided a more logical and systematic approach was required. There were seven symbols total on each wheel, and no wheel had the same symbol. So, I made a crude drawing of each of the twenty-one markings and started working my way through one at a time. When one failed, I made a note of the sequence and tried the next.

Tracey, it has to be said, was not enamoured with my new acquisition, labelling it 'garish and ugly.' Everyone's entitled to an opinion, I suppose. It did not find pride of place in our living room, and instead I gave it a home below my nightstand. Tracey quickly became annoyed at the amount of time I was spending trying to figure out the lock, thinking it a waste of time. To keep the peace with her, I took to working on the puzzle at night while she slept beside me. After my failed attempts, I would sleep.

And that was the first time I remembered having those vivid dreams. Or, rather, nightmares. Horrible regurgitations of the mind; random thoughts expelled from the subconscious with, seemingly, no real meaning. But then I had a similar dream only three nights later. And then they occurred more frequently. Each was unique, but the fear and dread were unmistakable constants.

In these dreams, I was never myself. And I don't mean that I felt 'off' or 'not my usual self.' I mean to say that I was a completely different person, looking through a stranger's eyes—strangers from different countries, and even different periods of time. In one dream, I was a black man, huddled by candlelight in my small room, filled with far too many people. I knew I was a slave. How I had come across the box, I did not know, but at night I sat by the small window, looking out at the plantation before me, and worked feverishly to open the box while the others who shared my fate slept and regained their strength. The entire time I worked on the box, I felt like I was being watched. Fear settled deep in the pit of my stomach, and I cast nervous glances from the window. On more than one occasion, I was sure I saw someone, always at the edge of my gaze. But, when I focused, there was no one there. Either the shadows claimed him—I was sure it was a *him*—or he had never been there in the first place. I even got the impression he was completely naked.

In another dream, I was in an East Asian country. Japan, I thought, kneeling on the floor of a hut in silky robes. Again, I worked on the same box, and again I failed to find out what was hidden within. The sliding doors before me were open, the warm night air rolling in and cooling my face. Beyond my home was a line of trees, and there, again, I saw him—a little clearer this time, but still always in my peripheral vision. As far as I could tell he was definitely naked, but with a horrible red scar down his middle. On his head I could see no face at all, just a blank expanse of skin. He had no hair that I could see, either.

I had been an English Lord, an Irish immigrant, and a thug from the ghetto, amongst others, and in every dream I was trying to solve that damn puzzle and open the box. And in every dream, I failed.

And he watched.

I knew that the dreams about this object meant that it was eating into my subconscious, yet I could not explain that. It was troubling. But not enough to make me dispose of the box. Indeed, it seemed to strengthen my resolve, and I pressed on, working my way through the possible sequences. I was determined to open this thing and claim its secrets.

As the days went on, Tracey commented that I was becoming more and more distant. I'd taken to tinkering with the thing during any free time I had, and it drove a wedge between us. My work as a freelance writer suffered, too—I missed deadlines, and the quality of my work took a nose-dive. Signs that this was getting out of hand were every-where, but I just ignored them.

The dreams soon became a nightly occurrence. Argu-ments with Tracey were almost as frequent. One night, about two weeks after buying the box, I was awake well past two in the morning toying with it. Tracey lay asleep beside me, snoring lightly. It was warm and clammy and, feeling hot, I set the box down on my nightstand and got to my feet to stretch my back. I felt uneasy. It was a feeling that was familiar to me, a sense of dread—the one I had when I dreamed. The one I had when *he* was watching.

But this was not a dream.

I moved towards the window. I didn't really want to look out, but I needed to see, to assure myself this was all in my head. Maybe then I could force myself to snap out of this needless obsession. I'd snapped earlier when Tracey had called it that—an obsession—but that's exactly what it was. I pulled back the curtains and peered out from the window, hoping to see an empty street, but actually expecting to see *him* standing there, motionless, watching me.

And that is exactly what I saw.

I wanted to scream, but my throat closed up, and nothing but a murmur escaped me. In my dreams, he was always on the periphery, always just out of plain sight. Now I could see his every hideous detail as he was drenched in the dull orange glow from the streetlight above him.

His face was hidden by an additional layer of pale, blotchy skin, pulled tight over his head like a mask. He stood perfectly still. His tall, hunched, and skeletal body— that looked almost insect-like—was littered with scabs and scars. The largest, most unsightly scar ran up his front, from the bottom of his stomach to the top of his chest. It looked like he had once been cut open and crudely sewn back up with sinew. And, as if to cap off his obvious torture, there was an angry patch of scar tissue where his genitals should have been.

The room around me began to spin as a cold sweat ran from my brow. My knees buckled.

I fell.

I would guess that I passed out before I hit the floor, as I don't remember the contact.

Tracey found me in a heap the next morning. She shook me awake, and I remember looking up at her, seeing her expression of concern. Though it wasn't the first thing I remembered that morning. The image of *him* standing outside my home was seared into my mind, and it was my first thought before I'd even opened my eyes.

'I'm scared,' was all I managed to say to Tracey, and I began to weep. She was obviously confused, but did not question anything. She just hugged me. We sat like that for a long while.

~

Later that day, Tracey and I talked about what had happened, but of course I lied. How could I tell her the truth? It was insane to even think about. Instead, I told her that I had simply got up to get some water, felt light-headed, and must have passed out. She worried for me, naturally, and insisted I visit the doctor to make sure everything was okay. I agreed. Then she asked me why I had told her I was scared. I lied again and told her I didn't remember saying that.

I couldn't explain what was going on, but I knew something was not right, not natural. Instead of going to the doctor that day, as I'd promised Tracey, I went back to that charity shop.

The woman who had so easily conned me out of my money wasn't there this time, replaced instead by an old man who I initially took to be her husband.

'Morning,' he said, greeting me with a wave.

'Good morning,' I replied. I tried to sound as pleasant as I could, but I was wary of him. If he was anything like his wife, I had no doubt that I would leave this shop another fifty pounds lighter. 'I was hoping to speak to the lady who served me about a fortnight ago.'

'Ah, that would be Claire,' he said. 'Young lady with black hair?'

I shook my head. 'No, this was a more... senior lady,' I

replied, careful with my wording. 'She was quite thin, and I seem to recall she had a slight blue rinse in her hair.'

The man looked confused. 'No one of that description works here,' he said. 'Not anymore.'

'That can't be right,' I said.

'I'm telling you, it is,' he replied, almost angrily, and got to his feet. 'There are only two people who work here. Myself, and a young volunteer. You must be mistaken.'

'This doesn't make sense,' I went on. 'I was here, two weeks ago, and bought an old wooden box. It was a Sunday.'

'We don't open Sundays,' he stated. 'I'm afraid you are wrong. We do not open on Sundays, and the woman you are describing most certainly did not serve you. I'm starting to think this is some kind of twisted prank.'

'But-'

'No buts,' he shouted, interrupting. 'Will you please leave? I'll not listen to any more of this. If you do not leave, I'll call the police.' Tears were welling up in his eyes.

'Look, I can show you the box if you want. It was wooden, as I say, with strange carvings on it. It has a combination lock, but I haven't been able to open it yet.'

'Lies,' he screamed, shaking his fist. He was unsteady on his feet. 'Get out. Get out now, I tell you, or I'll throw you out myself.'

He came at me and I backpedalled, not wanting an altercation. I doubted he would be capable of causing me harm, but I certainly didn't want to accidentally hurt him whilst defending myself. I left the shop as he shouted angrily at me with stringy spittle leaping from his mouth. The tears that had begun to well were now streaming down his face.

～

Even though I knew something was very wrong, thoughts of opening that box had burrowed deep into my brain like some kind of botfly larvae. Always there, wriggling, and sending out infectious thoughts that I could not ignore. And so, whenever I was alone, I kept on trying the combination lock, working my way through the different sequences.

And still the dreams persisted. Still *he* showed up outside of my house. It was terrifying to see him—always at night—standing perfectly still. And it was impossible to see if he was looking directly at me, as his face—if he had one—was completely hidden, though I was certain I could see the shape of his mouth move beneath the hood of skin.

He seemed to be screaming silently.

He would stand still for as long as I looked at him, but if I averted my gaze for a moment, he would disappear completely. And I never once saw him move.

~

Last night, I had another dream, which revealed some crucial information to me. In this dream, I was a rugged, bearded fellow, living out in the wilderness in a cabin. I was seated at a self-made table in my bedroom, with a mirror on the wall just above me. In my hands, I held the box. I thumbed the wheels to form the sequence I wanted, a sequence that I was sure would work. I had the vague idea that I had seen it somewhere before. Was it in a dream? A dream within a dream?

I rolled the first wheel into the correct position. Then the second. With my breath held, the last wheel fell into place, and I heard a click. As I began to open the box, I looked to the mirror before me.

He was standing behind me.

The faceless man.

I awoke screaming in fright as soon as I saw him in the mirror. I looked around, panicked, and found myself alone in my room, with Tracey now sleeping at her parents'. But, thankfully, the sequence I'd used on the combination lock in that dream was still perfectly clear in my mind.

It is mid-morning now, and the house is mine alone. I am seated at my desk with the box in my hands. I shouldn't open it, I know that, but I also know that I will, and I can't explain why. The first two wheels are in their correct positions. One more turn of the last wheel and the box will open; I will finally find out what is inside. Surely then I will have answers. Some kind of explanation as to what has been happening to me.

This thing has to give me something.

I let the wheel click into position and feel a latch release.

He is behind me now. I can sense him. Almost feel him. I can also hear some kind of muffled breathing, and I detect a sudden odour of sulphur. It smells horrific.

'God forgive me,' I say aloud, and open the box...

THE DEMON ON THE FARM

4-1

Thomas Kerr
1679

Ellie heard the axe cut heavily into the wood as she approached Thomas. The older boy—who was very tall and well developed for his age—was making kindling for her father. It was one of Thomas' many tasks as a farmhand. She noted the look of concentration on his face, and that his cotton shirt had grown damp with sweat. Still, he did not slow or pause in his efforts.

Chop, chop, chop.

It was warm outside on the farm, with only a gentle breeze to help cool the hired workers that toiled away. There were many people here on a daily basis, most of whom would return to their own homes later in the evening, but the farm was young Ellie Dunton's home.

'Hello, Thomas,' the little blonde girl said, skipping towards her friend. She had two slices of buttered bread in her hands. Thomas stopped his work and turned to her.

'Morning, Miss Ellie,' he replied with a big smile. 'How are you today?'

'Fine, thank you.' She sat on a large log close to where Thomas was working and bit into one of the slices of bread.

She held the other out towards him. 'Want some?' she asked through a mouthful of food.

He looked at her with a frown, then back to the main house.

'I don't know, Miss Ellie,' he said.

'Don't worry,' she told him. 'Father and Mother have gone to the Johnstones' today. They won't find out. Come.' She patted the space beside her. 'Sit.'

With a little reluctance, Thomas moved and sat beside her, his large frame dwarfing her. He had just turned eighteen, Ellie knew, but looked much older. She smiled as he bit down into the bread. His first bite was timid but then, as the taste of the generous butter hit, he began to gobble it down. She giggled.

'Oi!' a voice shouted.

Ellie knew immediately who had yelled over to them. The young male tones belonged to her brother, Andrew. She looked up and saw that he, as well as her older sister, Alice, were both walking over to them. Ellie saw Thomas tense up.

'Don't worry,' she said to him, then turned to her approaching siblings. 'What do you want?'

'Why are you talking to *him*?' Andrew asked her.

'He's my friend,' Ellie answered, getting to her feet.

'Well, he shouldn't be,' Andrew replied. He and Alice stopped before them. Alice was twirling a lock of her hair around a finger.

'And why not?' Ellie asked, and planted her hands on her hips.

'Cos Father wouldn't like you befriending the hired help.'

'Don't care,' Ellie said. 'He's my friend and that's all there is to it.'

'Well, maybe I'll tell on you. Wonder what Father will

say when he finds out you've been feeding this idiot our bread?'

Thomas stared at the ground.

'He is not an idiot,' Ellie said and stepped forward, prodding Andrew in the chest. 'And if you tell on me, then I'll tell Father that you have been stealing milk. I saw you do it. And he'll believe me, anyway. He always believes me.'

'You'll keep your mouth shut,' Andrew said, and stepped closer to Ellie. She didn't back down.

'Oh stop it, both of you,' Alice said, stepping between them. 'Andrew, you won't say anything, so stop teasing. But Ellie, you shouldn't be giving Thomas bread like that. If others find out he's had more than his share, they won't be happy.'

'I'm sorry, Miss Alice,' Thomas said.

'It's fine, Thomas,' she said. 'Anyway, come on, Andrew. It's too hot out here. I want to go inside.'

Andrew huffed, but turned and walked away. 'Fine. See you later, Ellie,' he said with annoyance in his voice. He then added, 'And see you, too, *idiot*.'

'*You're* the idiot,' Ellie shouted back. As the two siblings moved away, she again sat next to Thomas. The large boy looked sad, even on the verge of tears.

'Don't listen to him,' she said, rubbing his large arm. 'He's just mean.'

'He's right, though.'

'No, he isn't.'

Thomas slowly got to his feet.

'I have to go.'

'Where?'

'I have work to do over in the mill,' he answered, and looked over to the far end of the grounds. Ellie followed his gaze to the stone corn mill. Circular and tall, it rose up out of the ground like a small tower. Fatter at the base, thinning out towards the top.

'I'll let you get back to it, then,' she said, then noted another look on his face. It wasn't just sadness. There was something else there, too. 'What is it?' she asked him.

'I don't really like that place,' he said.

'Why?'

He shrugged. 'You wouldn't believe me.'

'I would,' she said, and stood up. 'Tell me.'

Thomas shook his head. 'It's nothing. Just sometimes I think I hear...' he trailed off.

'What?' she asked.

'Nothing,' he finally said with a shake of his head. 'I have to go, Miss. Ellie. Sorry if I got you in trouble.'

Ellie watched the older boy trudge over to the stone mill and dearly wanted to know what was troubling him about that place. For one, she considered him her friend, even if she wasn't supposed to, but there was more to it than that. The mill scared her, too.

When playing near it, she often heard voices inside when there should have been no one there. Voices, and a horrible cackling. Like a low, evil laugh.

And only last night, after waking from a nightmare, she'd looked out of her bedroom window, and could have sworn she saw a shadowy figure standing outside of it.

Her brother, Andrew, had once told her that mill was haunted. He said that many work-hands had died inside it over the years. Alice argued it was just a story, but Ellie had to wonder...

She hoped Thomas would be safe in there.

Thomas felt scared, being in this place again. He also felt bad for the young Dunton girl. For reasons he couldn't understand, Ellie was always nice to him. But, just for the simple act of being her friend, he had almost gotten her into trouble. Andrew may have been mean, as Ellie had said, but he was right about Thomas.

Thomas was an idiot. At least he was smart enough to know that.

And he'd always been an idiot, too. Even his father had said as much, before he'd left both Thomas and Thomas' mother for good. So, if Thomas couldn't use his brains, he had decided he would use his brawn to help provide a little for his dear mother, and he was thankful for the meagre job here at the farm that Edward Dunton—Ellie's father—had given him.

Which was why he carried out all of his duties without question and to the best of his abilities. Like now, inside the corn mill, cleaning the mechanisms and bagging the corn.

It was hard work, that strained his back, and the heat and near-dark made things oppressive in here. So he jammed the door of the mill open to allow in some sunlight. But the shadows were still dominant.

Thomas wanted to be done quickly, and so he worked hard, concentrating all of his focus on what he was doing, and trying to block out the memories of what had happened in here before.

Besides, that had all been in his head. It hadn't been real. Couldn't have been. He told himself that again. A reassuring thought. But one he didn't quite believe.

The light waned from outside, and it took Thomas a moment to realise the door was slowly closing of its own accord. The squeak of the hinges alerted his attention to it, and Thomas saw the door close fully, blocking out all light.

Leaving him in darkness.

He cried out as the memories of what had happened before now sprang up in his mind. He ran through the darkness to the thick wooden door and heaved at it, but it would not move.

Wouldn't even budge.

Not again, not again, not again.

'Let me out,' he yelled. He could hear the panic in his own voice. He banged at the door. 'Let me out!'

Thomas felt a cold breath on his neck. A horrible, rotting smell overwhelmed his senses, and the feeling of an icy gust on his skin caused Thomas to stiffen up in fright.

He then heard that horrible—almost otherworldly—chuckle. It seemed to come from the space all around him, rather than one specific point.

Thomas quickly turned and pressed his back against the door, pushing himself into the thick timber as hard as he could. He could see nothing but darkness before him.

The laughter continued.

Something was here in the mill with him. He knew it. Something that was not human.

'Who's there?' he asked in a quivering voice.

Whatever it was, the thing was now directly before him. Thomas could feel its presence. He then felt something long and spindly take hold of his throat, and he gasped.

'What are you?' Thomas wheezed out.

It answered him, as it had before, and whispered things into his ear. Horrible things. Ungodly things.

Things it wanted Thomas to do.

And the sickening utterances were becoming harder and harder to ignore.

4-4

Ellie had noticed a change in her friend, Thomas, over the last few days.

He didn't look like he was sleeping much, and bags were prominent under his eyes. His skin had paled considerably.

She had tried talking to him, only yesterday, but he'd just ignored her completely. He'd even ignored Andrew when the boy tried to tease him, concentrating only on the job at hand with a focused intensity. Thomas simply went on chopping wood, with a hint of a smile on his face, as Andrew grew tired of his failed goadings.

Chop, chop, chop.

Thomas spent a lot of time in the corn mill as well, which surprised Ellie, considering what he'd told her about that place. She was worried about him.

Now she lay on her bed, readying herself for sleep, but was unable to switch off her mind. What had caused the sudden change in Thomas?

The wind howled outside.

Even though it was the middle of summer and the nights had gotten warmer, over the last few days a noticeable cold had set in. It rained more, and the wind seemed to be building up to a storm.

Ellie didn't really want to sleep. Her nightmares had grown worse recently, and with them came a horrible feeling of foreboding.

She closed her eyes and tried to ignore the wind, hoping sleep would soon come and claim her for the night. But it was no good. The sandman eluded her. Her mind was simply too active.

She kept thinking of poor Thomas, and of ways she could help him through whatever troubles he was having that he would not share with her. She also thought about the mill. That place frightened her.

She sat up in bed, not really knowing why, just overcome with an urge to look out of the window towards the mill. Perhaps to reassure herself that all was as it should be. That nothing was out there lurking in the night. So she stood and walked to the window and looked out.

All was not as it should be.

The door to the mill was wide open, and someone was standing just outside, shirtless, in the night. Someone she recognised.

Thomas.

His pale skin stood out against the darkness. He was motionless. Worse still, Ellie was certain she could see something moving within the shadowed depths of the mill. She saw eyes.

Lots of eyes.

She wanted to scream. Then she saw Thomas move. His head twisted up to look at her, and his smile seemed full of malevolence.

'But I'm telling the truth, Mum,' Ellie said, stomping her foot.

'I'm sure you are, sweetheart,' her mother replied without looking at her daughter. Ellie's mother was barely listening, concentrating instead on her cooking. The large kitchen smelled of freshly baked bread. 'But I'm busy at the moment. I'll speak to your father about this later.'

Ellie sensed she would get nowhere with this conversation.

She'd tried to tell her mother what she had seen the previous night—Thomas standing outside of the mill, when he should have been at home. And of that thing behind him in the shadows.

But her mother either didn't believe her, or wasn't interested.

'What will Father do?' Ellie asked.

'Speak to Thomas, I suppose,' her mother said, busy kneading dough for a fresh batch of bread.

'Will Thomas get into trouble?'

Her mother shrugged. 'I don't know, Ellie. Now please, I need time to get everything ready. Your father and I are going over to the Johnstones' tomorrow evening and I still have a lot to do.'

The Johnstones lived a few miles away, but Ellie's parents went there often when local dignitaries gathered for their regular get-togethers. That meant her parents would be out for most of the night, not returning until the early hours of the morning.

That idea didn't sit well with Ellie. It wasn't uncommon for the children to be left alone, as Alice—the oldest at sixteen—was seen as mature enough to look after the younger siblings.

Normally, Ellie would have looked forward to a night of playing with her brother and sister, as well as Alice's more relaxed attitude when it came to bedtime. But not now.

The idea of her parents being away for most of the night now made her feel scared and vulnerable.

'Do you have to go?' Ellie asked.

'Yes,' her mother said, in a matter-of-fact tone.

Ellie paused, considering her next words. 'Can't you miss it, just this once?'

'Whatever for?' Only now did her mother look over to Ellie.

'I'm scared,' Ellie said. 'I don't want you to go.'

'Don't be silly, Ellie,' her mother admonished. 'Now run along. I'm busy, and don't have time for this nonsense.'

'But Mum—' Ellie began, but her mother cut her off.

'No, Ellie,' she said, sternly. 'Now go.'

Ellie stomped her foot again, defiantly, but knew her mother would not be swayed. She left the kitchen and stepped outside into the warm afternoon sun. She looked over and saw Thomas, yet again chopping up wood.

He looked over to her and smiled.

Chop, chop, chop.

Ellie slept uneasily that night, constantly on edge. Every now and again she would peek from the window to see if Thomas was again lurking outside.

Her plan, if she did see him, was to race to her parents' room and wake them. They would then fix everything. And at least they were home tonight. Tomorrow they would be away, leaving Ellie and her siblings alone.

Her father had said he would speak with Thomas, but Ellie wasn't sure if he had gotten around to it yet.

However, though she checked constantly, Thomas never made an appearance. And, eventually, Ellie succumbed to exhaustion and fell asleep, unaware that Thomas was waiting patiently inside of the dark mill.

Alone with the shadows. And that *thing*. The one that continued to whisper to him, eroding the last of his resistance and conscience.

~

Ellie spent most of the next day struggling with her problem. On the one hand, she wanted to keep away from Thomas as much as she could, but then again, she was supposed to be his friend.

And she prided herself on being a good friend.

So, she determined to try to talk with him again and find out what was wrong. She'd always liked him, and even felt sorry for the teasing he went through just because he wasn't the cleverest of boys. But now she felt something different.

The way he had been acting recently made her afraid of him.

But, despite this, she resolved to at least reach out to him. What sort of friend would she be if she couldn't do that?

Later in the afternoon, she went outside to find him. Other farmhands worked away, but she could not see Thomas. He certainly wasn't at his usual position: chopping wood by the log. In fact, the axe was nowhere to be seen, either.

After a brief look around, she concluded there was only one place he could be. A place she didn't want to go to. But she went, anyway.

Ellie approached the mill cautiously, straining her ears to pick up any noises from within. The mill itself was some distance from the main body of the farm, and the closer she got, the more the everyday noises made by the other farmhands diminished. It made her feel isolated.

Ellie soon approached the door to the mill and stood before it, listening carefully. She couldn't hear anything.

At first.

Then she heard whispering. Two distinct voices. One, she was certain, was Thomas. The other she couldn't place. The voices were low, and not clear enough to understand.

Then, the mysterious, unknown voice died away, leaving only Thomas, who repeated one word over and over again. One that eventually became clear to Ellie.

'Kill, kill, kill.'

Ellie felt a sudden pang of fear and turned and ran as fast as she could back to the house. She knew she had to tell her parents what she'd heard. Surely they couldn't ignore this?

Her lungs burning at the effort of prolonged sprinting, Ellie burst into the kitchen, only to see Alice and Andrew sitting at the table.

'Where is Mother?' she asked, panting. 'I need to speak to her.'

'What's wrong, sister?' Andrew asked. 'You look like you've seen a ghost.'

'I need to speak to Mother. Or Father. Where are they?' Ellie raised her voice, demanding an answer.

'What's gotten into you?' Alice asked.

'Just answer me!' Ellie was shouting now.

'They've left,' Alice said. 'Gone to the Johnstones'.'

'Already?'

'Yes, already. Now what is going on?'

'We need to go after them,' Ellie said.

'Don't be ridiculous,' Alice answered dismissively.

'What is wrong with you, anyway?' Andrew asked. 'You're acting very strangely.'

'It's Thomas.'

'What about him?' Alice asked.

'Yeah, what has the idiot done now? Cut off his own arm?' Andrew chuckled at his own tasteless joke.

'Something *is* wrong with him,' Ellie stressed.

'I could have told you that,' Andrew chuckled.

'No,' Ellie went on, 'something is *really* wrong with him. I think he is planning to hurt us.'

'What makes you say that?' Alice asked, finally sounding serious.

'Yeah, I thought the big idiot was your friend?' Andrew chipped in.

'He is, but...' Ellie didn't know how to put her concerns into words. At least, not believable ones. 'I heard him, in the mill. He was talking to someone, but there was no one inside with him. He kept saying the word kill, over and over again.'

'Oh come on now, Ellie,' Alice said, shaking her head. 'I'm sure you misheard. Thomas is a nice boy. He would never hurt us.'

'No, I didn't mishear, Alice. Whatever is in the mill, the ghost or whatever, it's in his head now.'

Both Alice and Andrew sniggered.

'There isn't anything in the mill, sister,' Andrew said.

'But you said it was-'

'Haunted?' he cut in. 'I wasn't serious. There is no such thing as ghosts. I was only saying it to scare you.'

'See, Andrew?' Alice admonished. 'See what your stories do?' She turned to Ellie. 'Now look, Ellie, this is all just a misunderstanding.'

'But he's been acting so odd.'

'That may be,' Alice went on. 'But that doesn't mean he is possessed and means to kill us. Now, the workers will all be going home soon, Thomas as well, and it will just be us. So there is nothing to be scared of.'

'But-'

'No buts, Ellie. Now, go and play.'

Ellie started to protest again, but thought better of it. She knew she would get nowhere with it. Maybe her sister was right. The workers would be going home soon, so she would just have to make sure that Thomas left with them. She turned and walked from the room, but she heard Andrew chuckling as she left.

'That's your fault,' she heard Alice say to him.

Was it true? Had she let her mind run away with itself? If so, what kind of friend did that make her to Thomas?

A terrible one.

However, she couldn't shake the feeling in her gut, or forget the smile on his face as he worked with his axe. Or what she was certain she'd heard him say in the mill.

Kill, kill, kill.

If the wind had been howling during previous nights, then tonight it positively roared, accompanied by a fierce rain that pelted down from above.

The front and back doors of the farmhouse, though latched shut and locked, rocked and rattled in their frames.

Andrew was in his element, insisting they all tell ghost stories by candlelight, but Alice didn't think it was a good idea. According to her, Ellie wasn't in the best frame of mind to hear them. Andrew had called Ellie a chicken, so Ellie had told him to tell his scariest one, determined to prove him wrong.

And so he did.

Ellie was regretting it now as he regaled them with a local legend of how the first settlers of Bishop's Hill had all died in a very violent and mysterious manner—cut open and decapitated by one of their own.

Alice was disinterested. Ellie tried to act like she wasn't scared. And Andrew made sure to dwell on every gruesome detail.

Then Alice screamed.

Both Ellie and Andrew spun around to see what had scared her so. Outside the kitchen window, standing in the pouring rain, axe in hand and manic grin spread across his face, was Ellie's friend.

Thomas.

'What do you want?' Andrew yelled, trying to compose himself and sound as imposing as he could.

Thomas didn't answer. He simply raised the axe and brought it crashing down through the glass, sending shards of it spilling to the floor inside. The wind and rain poured through.

Ellie and Alice screamed as Thomas climbed in through the window. He ignored the broken glass still protruding from the frame. Ellie saw it cut into the large boy and draw blood as he clambered through, uncaring of the pain, and stood up to his imposing full height.

Andrew grabbed the iron kettle from the stove and hurled it at Thomas. It struck its target, connecting with his face, and knocked Thomas back a few steps. Thomas, however, only shook his head, his nose now bent, and smiled.

His teeth were black.

As her heart raced, Ellie felt someone grab her hand. It was Alice, who then dragged her from the room.

'Andrew,' Alice called, 'run!'

Andrew obeyed, and the three of them ran upstairs, pursued by the larger boy, whose heavy footsteps thumped up the stairs behind them.

The three fleeing siblings ran into Alice's bedroom and slammed the door shut. They managed to close it just as the brute giving chase rammed into the other side. The force of the impact knocked them all back a step, but Andrew and

Alice managed to adjust themselves and pressed back against the door, screaming.

'Ellie!' Alice shouted. 'Hide. Now.'

Ellie obeyed, terrified for her life, and crawled under Alice's bed as her two older siblings pushed against the door with all their might, struggling to keep the boy outside.

The sound of an axe hitting the wood of the door startled them all. They screamed again.

Thunk, thunk, thunk.

The axe cut a long gap into the wood, and Ellie could see Thomas through it. He worked relentlessly, and his eyes were manic, wild... possessed.

'Leave us alone,' Alice yelled. She pressed against the door that was being hacked away, desperate to not let him in.

The axe came through again... and this time struck flesh. Alice howled as the sharp blade buried itself into her right arm at the wrist. Blood spilled free. Andrew screamed her name. Ellie's bladder relieved itself as she cried.

The axe wiggled, and pulled free, but Alice still desperately pushed back against the door, knowing that if she relented, then they would all die. The axe came down again, this time lopping her hand off completely. Alice cried out in agony and fell back to the floor. She clutched the bloody stump at the wrist as blood pumped from it, spurt after spurt of horrible crimson liquid.

Andrew ran to her side, tears streaming down his face.

Ellie heard a loud crash and saw that Thomas had kicked the door open. The wind picked up even more, becoming deafening, and lightning flashed. In that bright streak, Ellie saw something standing behind Thomas in the hallway.

An indescribable, evil thing.

It wasn't human. Couldn't be.

She squealed.

This was a nightmare she couldn't wake up from. A nightmare that was about to get worse. Thomas entered the room. As he did, Andrew jumped to his feet and launched himself at the larger boy, crying out in fury. They wrestled, but Andrew soon found himself overpowered. Thomas pushed him back and raised the axe. He twisted it in his grip and brought down the heavy handle to strike Andrew on the top of the head with the thick shaft. Ellie heard an audible crack, and Andrew fell to the floor, his whole body convulsing.

'Thomas, please!' Alice screamed, but the boy walked up to Andrew's fallen body and held the axe high again.

The sharp edge now aimed down.

Thomas swung.

Ellie heard the dull, wet sound of impact as Thomas buried the axe into Andrew's head. The boy didn't even have a chance to scream. His body twitched and spasmed. Thomas pulled the weapon free, and swung again, this time cutting into Andrew's neck. Blood spat from the flesh and streaked the floor. Andrew gurgled.

And Thomas carried on with his dreadful work.

Chop, chop, chop.

Ellie couldn't be sure at what point Andrew died, but his body became a mangled, chopped-up mess. Thomas concentrated his strikes around the younger boy's head, neck, and upper body. The throat was cut through so much that Andrew's head was now connected only be a few strands of meat.

Alice, still cradling her arm, was begging for her life. She backed herself up against the bed that little Ellie had hidden beneath. Ellie could smell nothing but the sharp, metallic odour of blood in the air. It was overpowering.

Thomas, seemingly finished with Andrew, then walked over to Alice. The girl pleaded and screamed.

Thomas didn't utter a single word as he swung the axe at her. The blow came in sideways and connected with Alice's head, into the jaw of her open mouth. Whist the weapon was lodged into her, Thomas used it to pull Alice away from the bed and drag her next to her deceased brother. He then set about Alice again with the axe, mutilating the girl's upper body, like he had done with Andrew, and turning her face into a mass of red pulp.

Finally, he turned his attention to Ellie.

He stomped towards her and reached under the bed. She kicked and screamed, but he easily pulled her free, dragging her over to lie beside her siblings.

'Please, Thomas. Please, just stop,' Ellie begged. She felt the blood that covered the floor soak through her clothes.

Thomas dropped the axe to the floor, dug into his pocket, and pulled out a knife. He smiled—another horrible, demonic grin—and raised the blade. Ellie closed her eyes, awaiting the inevitable.

'Please, Thomas,' she said. 'Please don't do this.'

After a few moments—when nothing had happened—she opened her eyes again and saw, through tear-blurred vision, Thomas standing above her. The blade was still held aloft, but he didn't strike. His face was screwed up, the menacing smile gone, replaced by a look of conflict.

Maybe she had gotten through to him?

'Please, Thomas,' she repeated. 'I don't want to die. I'm scared. Please, don't hurt me.'

Ellie's pleas continued, and, eventually, Thomas actually lowered the knife. Tears began to form in his eyes, and they fell from his cheeks. He looked at the blade, like it was a foreign object, then to Ellie.

'I'm sorry,' he whispered. 'I'm so, so sorry.' He then turned and slowly walked from the room. Ellie was terrified, but clung to the hope of survival that had just appeared. Thomas walked out into the hallway.

Ellie closed her eyes, not wanting to look at the surrounding carnage. Then she heard a voice. It wasn't that of Thomas. This was someone else.

Some*thing* else.

'*Go back, thou hateful wretch, resume thy cursed knife. I long to view more blood. Spare not the young one's life.*'

Ellie looked over to the doorway and saw Thomas in the hall. Something was standing in front of him, blocking his way.

That thing.

That *demon*.

The very sight of the inhuman thing terrified Ellie to her core. Thomas turned back. That horrible smiled had returned.

Ellie wept as her former friend walked back over to her, raised the knife, and got to work.

Thomas sat on the same log he'd sat on with Ellie only days before.

He was crying. The guilt and horror—and the revulsion for himself—were overwhelming.

What had he done?

He couldn't stop replaying the scene over and over again in his mind. He'd watched as everything had happened, but could do nothing to stop it. Or, rather, he didn't want to stop it, despite knowing it was wrong.

Because it felt so right.

He had to obey the thing from the mill. He'd tried to resist it at first, but it had just returned, again and again, and dug further into his head, burrowing deeper. After a while, he couldn't disobey it.

Even now, as he was buried in guilt, Thomas could still sense that demon's presence. Both on the farm and, more troubling, actually within him, coiling around his very soul.

He remembered how poor Ellie had cried, how scared she had been, before he had thrust the knife into her. He saw her eyes open wide in pain one so young should never feel. Ellie had known what was coming, but still looked surprised. She hadn't had time to prepare for the feeling of death.

Thomas looked up. He could hear the clip-clopping of horses and the rolling of wheels over dirt. He saw the carriage approach the farm.

Mr. and Mrs. Dunton were returning.

Thomas could smell the blood of their children on him. They would find him here, and then find what remained of their children... and that would be it for him.

Thomas wasn't a smart boy, but he knew what happened to killers.

'Thomas?' he heard a voice say. 'What are you doing here? What is that you have on you?' It was Mrs. Dunton. He looked up, his eyes meeting her own. She looked confused. Then she made sense of the red stains that coated him. He saw the recognition in her eyes as she pieced together what it all meant.

Mrs. Dunton began to scream.

$\sim$

After being sentenced, Thomas died in agony. Imprisoned in a metal cage, he was left naked and exposed to the elements. Spikes from his steel prison pointed inwards and pierced into his skin. One was even wedged into his open mouth.

Crows pecked and feasted on his dying body.

When they got to work on his face, he screamed out loud and whipped his head from side to side. But the iron spike in his mouth did not budge, and he felt his jaw dislocate.

More agony.

It took days for poor Thomas to pass from this world.

But when he finally did, he realised the demon from the farm was not even close to being done with him.

4-9

Margaret Hobbes
1866

Margaret was tired.

She had been walking all evening, desperate to put as much distance as she could between her and... *him*.

Her ageing body ached.

The sky, that had only recently burned a deep, late-afternoon red, had now given way to the night, and stars pinpricked the black expanse above. Margaret was bruised and sore. She still hurt from the latest attack from her drunken husband.

Robert had come home, full of booze, and dragged Margaret to their small bedroom. He had thrown her to the bed and climbed atop her, promising a night to remember. She would rather he not have bothered, but let him have his way all the same. However, as had happened before, *little Robert* remained flaccid and uncooperative.

Margaret knew she could say nothing to console her husband and, as predicted, he flew into a violent rage and blamed her for his impotence. Robert proceeded to strike and choke her, as savagely as he ever had. Fearing for her life, Margaret waited until he'd fallen asleep and fled.

She didn't know where she would go, but knew that she needed to be away from him. And for good this time. After a lifetime of abuse, she made a decision that she should have made a long time ago. There would be no going back this time. He would no doubt come looking for her, so she had to remain hidden.

And she would die before going back to him.

Margaret walked almost the entire length of Bishop's Hill, not really knowing where she was heading. She had no friends to call on anymore—Robert had seen to that—so she just continued to walk, pulling her threadbare cotton clothing tightly around her, trying in vain to ward off the cold.

She reached the village centre—which was desolate at this time of night—before the idea of heading to the old farm entered her head.

Dunton Farm, was it?

She'd heard about it, heard what had happened there all those years ago—the family that were killed, almost two centuries past. There were many stories about the farm, and of the strange and terrible things that had happened there in the intervening years. It now stood abandoned, falling into ruin. No one wanted anything to do with it.

Everyone in the area considered it a place where something was decidedly... off.

A dark place.

Which suited her just fine, right about now. She felt nothing but darkness in her heart. The thought of the shadows there swallowing her up and hiding her from the world seemed appealing. At the very least, it would be a place to go and get away from the bite of the cold. Somewhere to hide until she could get her mind in order.

Margaret trekked through the village and along the long

road out to the farm. Her legs ached, and her feet were sore. The cold seemed to seep into her very bones. She wanted to collapse, just drop to the floor to let sleep take her.

As enticing as the thought was, she knew she could not. It was far too cold out in the open, and she did not think she could survive a bout of pneumonia. Not at her age.

So, she persevered, and pushed on past the built-up area of the village centre and out towards the farmlands.

Out towards Dunton Farm.

She knew she was getting close when the fields became overgrown and unkempt, and soon she could make out the silhouette of the stone mill standing tall in the distance.

It called to her, drawing her close, like some ominous beacon in the night.

With nowhere else to go, and no one to turn to, she went to it.

Heeding the call.

Denton Farm was, as Margaret suspected, completely abandoned. Many structures—including the old farmhouse—still stood, but they were in a state of ruin and dilapidation. Still, it would be enough for her. Enough to keep her out of the cold while she decided what her next move would be.

The air was cold and the night dark as she stalked around the land. Almost instinctually, Margaret wanted to get familiar with her surroundings and decided that a quick survey, before retreating to the house, would be wise. Timber shelters and sheds were dotted around the overgrown field, but it was the tall, tower-like structure that had first caught her attention. Margaret was not the most educated of people, but she knew that this building was a mill, possibly for corn.

She also knew, deep down in her gut, that she didn't want to be anywhere near it. It gave off an ominous, imposing feeling. A place of cold and isolation.

So, though she walked the entirety of the grounds, she gave this building a wide berth. Satisfied that there was no one else using this place to hide out, Margaret made her way over to the derelict house.

The front door was securely locked; however, some of the windows had been put through, allowing her to gain access. There was still a chill inside, but at least the house afforded her protection from the worst of the biting night air.

Margaret toured the old house. Most of the furniture and belongings had long since been stripped out, but there were a few remnants of the lost years. Echoes of the past.

She found the odd piece of clothing, and even—in one of the bedrooms—a box of old jewellery, which she duly pocketed in hopes of selling.

The small trinkets she found—indications of lives previously lived—were few, and the house was otherwise very much bare. That only helped to reinforce the feeling of isolation Margaret had felt since walking onto the farm. In one of the bedrooms she also saw that a large portion of the timber floor was stained black.

It was extremely late, and she was exhausted. Satisfied that she was alone in the house, Margaret chose the largest bedroom available to sleep in that night. There were no beds, or anything comfortable to lie on, so the timber floor had to suffice. At least the floor to this room did not have a strange, faded black stain like the other room. A stain that looked—she feared—like old blood.

The night wore on, and Margaret struggled to sleep. Rest seemed to always be just out of her reach, leaving her exhausted but very much awake.

Lonely and in darkness.

Margaret had no idea of the hour when she first heard the noise. She sat upright and listened intently to make sure it was no trick of the mind.

A loud and sudden *thud*. Like a heavy footstep, coming from downstairs. Margaret's heart froze.

Could it be that there was someone on the ground floor? And, if so, did they know Margaret was here? But that couldn't have been. She'd checked *everywhere* in the house.

Another thought then sprang up in her mind: had Robert found her? If so, she knew that she was in very serious danger, and couldn't just wait here to be found. She slowly got to her feet, making as little sound as possible. Margaret kept herself low as she moved from the bedroom, onto the landing, and peered down the stairs. She heard the thumping footsteps again for a brief moment. They were moving from the living area to the entrance hallway directly below.

Thump, thump, thump.

Then, nothing. Quiet.

After a pause, they began yet again. Margaret's breath quickened. Surely Robert was down there. He had found her. It was the only explanation. She was surprised that he wasn't yelling and screaming for her to show herself.

The footsteps slowly thudded on, until Margaret noticed something was wrong. They sounded as if they had passed through from the living area and into the hallway below, stopping at the bottom of the stairs.

But no one was there. The hallway was empty, filled only with the darkness of the night.

Then, near silence. The only sound Margaret could hear was her own rapid breathing. It had to have been in her mind, she concluded. Had to be. All just her imagination. Margaret tried to keep herself calm, but she was losing that battle. She felt a panic rise.

Then, she felt a breath on her neck and detected a horrible, sour smell. Margaret turned and looked up.

She shrieked at the towering tall man that stood directly behind her. He looked down at her, and Margaret couldn't help but notice that his skin was pale, and his body was ravaged with scars. In addition, he had a jaw that hung unnaturally low, as if dislocated.

Fear gripped its icy fist around Margaret's heart, so tightly that she thought it might be the onset of a heart attack. She instinctively moved backwards and shrieked.

The man laughed as Margaret lost her footing and fell down the flight of stairs, knocking herself unconscious before she reached the bottom.

4-12

Margaret slipped in and out of consciousness for a while, but only remembered snippets. Darkness, eternal black, and that voice—inhuman, evil, and terrifying. It whispered obscenities to her. Vile things that turned her stomach.

The words invaded her subconscious, ideas that she could not shake, which wormed their way into her and nested—spreading their infected tendrils throughout her psyche.

As she came to, Margaret realised that she wasn't in the house anymore. She could sense that, but she had no idea where she was exactly. It was too dark to make anything out clearly. Margaret had no idea how long she had been in this place, wherever it was, as she had no idea how long she had been unconscious. All she knew was that she was cold, hungry, and in pain from the last thing she remembered clearly—falling down the stairs.

She remembered something else too.

That man.

The one in the house. The one that, she was certain, was not a living person at all.

Was she now dead, then? Was that man, the one with the ashen and torn skin, here to collect her soul and take her over to the other side? Is that where she now resided? In never-ending darkness, with whispers of evil as company?

Was this Hell?

For a time, Margaret thought it was, until a creeping light made itself known. At first, it was no more than a thin line. Then it slowly grew brighter, and the strengthening light pushed its way inward, revealing a wooden floor beneath her. Soon, Margaret saw that it was, in fact, sunlight, pushing its way in from beneath a thick wooden door.

She was not dead. This was not Hell. But where was she?

Margaret found her strength and slowly pushed herself to her feet. Her head pounded and her body was weak, but she managed to wobble over to the door. She fumbled with its handle and pushed it open.

Blinding light flooded her senses, enough that she had to cover her eyes and was forced to backpedal a few steps. After giving herself time to adjust, Margaret looked out to the world outside of this dark place and saw something she vaguely recognised. Something she had only seen previously in the darkness of night.

It was the farm. Dunton Farm.

She could make out the house up ahead. And that meant, she realised, she was now inside of the old mill that had so unsettled her.

As quickly as she could, Margaret scrambled from the building and out into the warm morning air. She continued farther away from it until her legs shook with exhaustion. Her lungs burned, screaming for breath, and she remembered the man from inside the house—*When was that, only a night ago? Longer?*—and also the voice from the mill.

And she remembered what it had told her.

There was something wrong with this place, with this farm, Margaret now knew. She was certain of it. She tried to search her memory, to remember the stories she'd heard about Dunton Farm, and what had happened here all those years ago. About the family that were murdered by the farmhand, Thomas Kerr. And what he had said before he was put to death. 'It was the Devil that made me do it!'

Was that what the thing from the mill was, then? The Devil?

And the man in the house... what did that make him?

But there was more to it, Margaret remembered. Other stories of this place, of the things people had seen over the years—strange figures stalking the land, and inhuman shrieks in the night.

She had thought they were just stories, designed to keep people away from this abandoned place. But now... she knew there was more to those legends.

With air once again in her lungs, Margaret ran, as fast as her body could manage, ready to leave this place behind. But, after passing the house and approaching the old road ahead, Margaret stopped.

Where would she go?

She couldn't go back to Robert. Not now, not after running away from him. Not ever. His anger would know no bounds, and it would likely be strong enough that he wouldn't hold back.

And would take the life from her body.

So, what then? She had no other friends to call on, and was still in the same situation that had brought her out here in the first place.

And she was alone.

She turned and looked back to the house. A strange

thought struck her. Would it really be so bad to stay here a little while longer? It was an idea that should have filled her with fear—should have scared her to the core—considering what she had experienced. In truth, it did scare her a great deal. But she could not deny that, for some reason, the notion held a certain kind of allure.

She thought about the idea of staying for a long while, with something whispering in her mind—a voice not her own, but one that was very persuasive—until the sun rose higher in the sky. Finally, Margaret walked back towards the house, her mind made up. She would stay here, for another night at least, until she could figure out what to do next.

And stay she did. The next night. And the next. And the next.

Margaret fed on whatever animals she could catch and cook—mostly vermin. Often, Margaret awoke in the mill, despite curling up the evening prior in one of the house's bedrooms. She often remembered her nightmarish dreams, and fragments of the whispers from that thing in the mill. A thing that, so far, had remained unseen.

Days turned into weeks which turned into months, and Margaret came to know this place as her home. She now knew that thing in the mill to be her master. And her master demanded things of her. Things that would have once turned her stomach and soured her soul.

But now... they sounded quite appealing.

Two months after first arriving at Dunton Farm, Margaret Hobbes took her first life.

4-13

The first one was easy. He was a young one.

A helpless one.

Margaret's master had demanded blood—demanded a life—and she was determined to find it. So, she set out late at night, when most were asleep, and wandered back into town. She was careful, making sure to avoid detection. When she reached a row of terraced houses near to the town centre, she tried a few doors. Many were unlocked. She would slip quietly inside and listen for signs of movement, and if the residents were still awake upstairs, making noise or talking, she would silently move on. In some houses, she found the residents sound asleep, but no suitable victim. Then, on her sixth try, Margaret found what she was looking for—a young child, sleeping on the ground floor, his parents upstairs.

And he slept heavily.

Margaret reached down and gently lifted him up before stealing him away—taking him from parents that would never again lay eyes upon him. The boy, heavy in her arms as she walked, did not wake until Margaret was clear of the town and on the final stretch of isolated road before she reached the farm.

Still groggy from sleep, he asked her who she was and where she was taking him. He seemed scared, too. Margaret smiled and told the boy that she was taking him somewhere nice. She also told him that his parents would be waiting for him when they arrived.

He seemed unsure of her response, but was obviously a good, well-mannered boy. He respected his elders and gave no further quarrel.

So, Margaret took him to the mill. Once inside—with only the moonlight from the open door to light their surroundings—the vile demon appeared, in all its hideous and inhuman glory.

The boy screamed in absolute terror. It was a fear so pure and so raw that it made Margaret giddy. She had thought the demon would kill the boy itself, but instead it ordered her to take his life instead. And it insisted she not spare the blood.

So, she obeyed, and took a large stone to the poor boy's head. Her master was pleased, but not sated—it needed more.

～

The second one took more effort, more planning, and was more prolonged. But it was a much more satisfying sacrifice.

One Margaret was proud of.

Knowing she needed to keep the monster in the mill satisfied, she soon decided on a target and formulated a plan to draw this person to the farm.

She left a note at her former home. One she knew would draw out Robert:

I know where she is. Meet me at the old Dunton Farm, tonight, in the mill. It will be open. Tell no one, and you will have her back... to do with as you will.

Predictably, Robert came, with all the rage she expected. It was past midnight when he stormed up to the mill. When he entered, he was shocked to see her standing there. His brief surprise soon turned to anger, and his face twisted into an animalistic scowl.

'Ungrateful wench,' he said through gritted teeth. Robert then balled up his fists; however, after taking just a single stride towards her, he stopped dead in his tracks. His face fell, the rage morphing into a look of horror.

Margaret could feel her master behind her, standing tall, looking down on this wretch who cowered before them. Margaret liked that—she liked seeing him in fear.

Robert made a move to run, but the door to the mill slammed itself shut, leaving only darkness. He screamed and tried to pull it open, but to no avail. There was an awful shriek—a sonic explosion of anger. An inhuman sound. Then, a large crash.

Near silence followed, only broken by the sound of Robert sniffling in pain. The door to the mill slowly opened again, letting in some of the moonlight from outside.

Margaret could now see Robert, lying on the floor, crying, his spine twisted at a horrible angle, legs trailing uselessly behind. She walked over to him, sneering down. Her master spoke to her and told her he would never raise his fist to her again. That he was helpless now.

Then, Margaret had an idea, and told Robert what she planned to do with him.

Over the course of several days, she fed him portions of arsenic, mixed in with his water. He could not move, or resist, only lie motionless in that mill, like a caged pet, as she forced him to sip down this poison. All with only the nightmarish demon to keep him company and torment him, driving the man to madness.

The arsenic provided a slow and painful death. Four days after being taken prisoner—and vomiting blood from the effects of the poison—Robert finally slipped into death.

Margaret enjoyed that.

However, her master was *still* not satisfied.

So she continued and gave the monster what it wanted, always careful with those she lured back, or stole away from their homes. All victims met a similar end—some poisoned, some bludgeoned, some gutted—and their bodies were stored up in the attic of the abandoned house, left to decompose and rot.

Children proved easiest to snare, and they were the ones her master enjoyed the most. Adults, mostly men, were more difficult for her. Margaret relied on trickery, sometimes promises of sex—even if her ageing body was not attractive to many—but she always managed to succeed.

And, importantly, to avoid discovery.

She stayed hidden on Dunton Farm, carrying out her evil deeds, for over a year.

Until one day, everything unravelled.

4-14

'I ain't giving up,' Tom Billington told his wife. His jaw was clenched, and he fidgeted with his fingers.

'But where else do we look?' Mary, his wife, asked.

'I don't know, but there has to be somewhere we haven't checked.'

Tom's younger brother, Eric, had been missing for three days now and that wasn't like him. Eric was the most responsible person Tom knew, and his brother's poor wife and children were now beside themselves with worry. Tom and Mary were seated at their small dining room table and he started to bite at his already painfully short fingernails. He wanted to go out looking for Eric, but Mary wasn't very enthusiastic about that idea. In fact, as far as Tom was concerned, she had been bloody difficult about it.

'Where would you go? People have searched everywhere already,' Mary reasoned.

'I don't know,' Tom replied, 'but there's gotta be some-place we haven't looked yet. I tell you, Mary, there is some-thing wrong with this town. How many people have gone missing recently? It ain't natural.'

'I know,' Mary agreed with a nod. She was fidgeting with her hands, as Tom had been—a sure sign of her unease. 'But you heard what the magistrate said. They think Eric has run off.'

'That's just not true, Mary,' Tom stated, shaking his head. 'You know it ain't. It's the same thing they say all the time, just because they can't explain what happened. Did all those little kiddies just run off, too? Some of them weren't even old enough to walk, for God's sake.'

Tom sighed and rubbed his face, feeling exhausted and exasperated in equal measure. Mary was, in many ways, the perfect wife, but right now he felt like he wasn't getting the support he needed from her.

But was that really fair? He had no idea where else they could look for his brother, so could he really be angry at Mary for not knowing more than he did? She was just trying to be reasonable.

Tom got to his feet. 'I'm going out.'

'To look?'

He nodded. 'Yes. I know what you're saying, Mary, and you're right. I don't know what to do. But I feel like I need to do something.'

'Don't go,' she pleaded, standing as well and grabbing his hand. 'Please.'

'I can't just sit here. I'll be back soon.'

He pulled away and headed to the front door.

'Then be careful,' Mary implored. Tom turned to face her and saw the worry evident on her face. He had a flash of realisation.

She was scared. Scared for him.

She didn't want him out there looking because she feared that whatever had happened to Eric—and to all the others who had gone missing—would happen to him, too.

He loved her for that. And he didn't want her to worry. But he couldn't just sit here while his brother was missing.

'I'll be careful,' he promised and stepped out into the night.

∽

Tom walked for hours that night, trying to think of the most remote parts of the town to search. The old woods were an option, but that would take him all night and, with no light at all, would likely turn up nothing. Maybe that could wait until morning.

Not that he hadn't searched there before.

He supposed he could go up to the farmlands on the outskirts of the town. There was that old, abandoned place out there: Dunton Farm.

It was another area he'd already been to, of course, and found nothing of interest. Though, at the time, Tom had thought he'd heard someone shuffling around upstairs, but after a thorough search of that floor, he'd turned up nothing and put it down to the wind. Dunton Farm was probably a half-hour walk from his current position, but if he was going to look somewhere, it was probably as good a place as any.

With a destination finally in mind, Tom set off.

∽

The last time Tom had been here, only a week before, he had been accompanied by a group of three friends, and it had been midday. It was a little creepy then, of course, as the place was overgrown and the buildings practically falling down. But other than that, there didn't seem to be anything out of the ordinary.

Now, however, in the dead of night, the farm seemed different. Much more ominous. And that damn mill, which stood silhouette against the moonlight, for some reason looked particularly threatening.

Tom walked quietly onto the property and over towards the house. The only sound he could hear was the light wind that blew around him. But, as he got closer to the building, he detected something else. Something different.

Whispering.

He looked up to a broken window and was certain the voice was coming from inside—from the floor above. He listened carefully, trying to make out what the feminine voice was saying.

It was repeating something, manically, over and over again.

'Show me more, I'll bring you more. Show me more, I'll bring you more. Show me more.'

Tom had known many strange people in his life, but when he heard this voice, he knew instantly he was listening to insanity. It chilled him. He pulled his coat tighter around himself.

Someone *was* here.

He felt his skin crawl, and the hairs on the back of his neck stood on end. Tom then looked to a broken window on the ground floor—the same one he'd used for entry the previous week—and knew he had to go in there again.

If someone was here, they might know what happened to Eric. Perhaps they were even involved, somehow.

He took a few steps towards the window, still listening to the demented whispers from up above. Until they stopped. He looked up and saw a figure looking back down at him.

A woman. Old and haggard with wide, wild eyes.

He saw her smile.

Then, he sensed a feeling of cold before him, directly ahead. He brought his gaze down and then let out a shriek. He backpedalled as quickly as he could, falling over his own feet, as the thing that stood inside the house reached out through the window for him.

Tom hit the ground, narrowly avoiding the grasp of the tall, pale man. The stranger was hideous: low hanging jaw, a grey body littered with painful gashes and scratches, and his face... it did not seem human.

Tom knew it *wasn't* human.

It leant forward again, reaching out again with an excited laugh. Tom screamed and scrambled backwards, away from the grasping hand. He then heard the woman up above cackle—a horrible and sinister sound.

Like that of a witch.

Tom ran and didn't look back. Didn't dare.

His legs ached, and his heart burned. And, on more than a few occasions, Tom thought he would pass out. But, regardless, he managed to run all the way back to his home.

And, once back, he tried to tell Mary what he'd seen, but the words would not come. Not coherently.

'I don't understand,' she kept saying. 'What is it? What did you see?'

'Something at the farm!' he yelled again. 'There's something there, Mary! Something evil! And I know that it took Eric!'

Mary was stunned and took over a minute to voice her next question. 'What do we do?'

Tom knew the answer to that.

Tonight, they could do nothing. Not on their own. But tomorrow, they needed help. They needed to round up the townspeople and do something he dearly didn't want to.

Return to the old farm and face that evil again.

Margaret heard the noise of the approaching crowd.

It was dusk, and she could see them through the upstairs window of the bedroom she'd made her own. The mob was a large one, and some of its group even had burning torches.

Which meant one thing—this was to be a lynching.

'Please, save me,' Margaret begged aloud to her horrific master. But the monster that she served now remained silent.

She heard yelling.

'Come out.'

'Show yourself.'

'What have you done with 'em?'

Soon, the raging group were upon the house, and they forced their way in through the front door. She knew that they would now find the bodies hidden in the attic, and that would be it for her.

'Please,' she begged again. 'If I'm dead, then I can't provide for you. I can't bring you anymore victims. Please, help me.'

But her master said nothing.

The mob made their way upstairs.

Margaret considered climbing up into the attic herself, as she had the last time people had been to search the farm —hidden amongst the rotting bodies. Though it was revolting, she had felt safe when nestled in amongst the decaying and cold corpses. That time, the group had not bothered checking the attic. Whether that was through laziness or incompetence, she wasn't sure. Didn't care. But now, she knew she would not be so fortunate.

The door to the bedroom was kicked open, stopping her from hiding anywhere, and a young man with a scraggly beard quickly spotted her. His eyes went wide.

Under different circumstances, this wretch would have made a perfect offering for the demon. Margaret could have even had a little fun with him and his cock herself... before slashing his throat.

'She's here!' he yelled, and others poured into the room with him.

'Who are you?' one man asked her, older than the first. Bigger, too. 'What's wrong with your face?'

'She looks like a demon,' another said.

No, she thought, *not quite*. She had seen the change in her appearance over the last few days when looking into one of the dirty mirrors that still remained in the house. It shocked her at first, but soon she came to think of it as a good thing. She was becoming more like her master.

'It's Margaret Hobbes,' someone shouted. 'She's been missing, too. I thought she was another victim.'

'That, or the one that's been taking people,' the first, scrawny man shouted.

Three men quickly grabbed Margaret, while others shouted an interrogation, yelling their questions. She remained silent. Even after a few slaps and punches, she did not dignify these lowly men with an answer.

She answered to only one being. A being far above these worthless bugs.

When they realised they would get nothing from her, the group then searched the house. For a while, Margaret thought they would yet again miss the attic completely—as stupid as they were—and perhaps be forced to leave her alone.

But one lout, who was obviously a little more observant than the others, spotted the hatch in the ceiling of the landing.

'Have we looked up there?'

They hadn't. So they did.

Upon seeing what was waiting up there, the horror and fury of the gathered men was absolute. Margaret was blamed instantly and beaten without mercy. She was then bound with rope and dragged from the house. The men told her that she would stand trial for what she'd done.

She didn't care. *Fuck 'em! Fuck 'em all!*

Margaret watched as they set fire to the house, their rage taking over. The bodies of the dead, it seemed, would be cremated right here and now.

Other buildings went up in flames, too. The whole place was now an inferno.

The mob even tried to set the mill alight. The home of the demon—her master—but it simply would not burn. After multiple failed attempts, the men left it, but turned their attention back to Margaret.

Some of the mob wanted to toss her into the flames— justice for the lives she'd taken, apparently. And it almost happened, too. She was dragged over to the blazing house and held close to the fire, but others overruled the notion, insisting she stand trial.

Margaret begged again to her master, praying for it to step in and help her. To save her life.

But she remained abandoned.

4-16

After a short trial—where Margaret did not even bother to speak to defend herself—she was taken to Durham City, to be hanged until dead.

Many people came out to see her execution. All normal citizens, so they would have everyone believe, who pretended to be good and decent, yet could not help but to eagerly watch the death of another. And they wore a smile while doing it.

Margaret was taken up onto the gallows, and a noose was placed around her neck. The crowd shouted and threw things. She didn't care. She served a higher entity. She was confident that, even in death, her master would protect her.

Then Margaret dropped, and she was dying. The noose strangled the life from her after her neck failed to snap completely.

She kicked and fought, her body reacting on impulse, trying to stave off the inevitable.

The crowd cheered.

And Margaret Hobbes passed from this world... and into another. As she did, the veil was lifted. All the despicable acts she had committed over the past year were fully brought to bear on her exposed conscience. No longer enthralled by that vile monster from the mill, her mind no longer clouded and confused, the horrific truth crushed her.

Those innocent people... and children.

And now, she was somewhere that did not make sense to her. Margaret had no body, no form, and existed in a way she could not understand.

The sky above her was a swirl of unnatural stars—an expanse that stretched on forever. The stars moved like they were living. And the landscape she stood on was a pulsating, living, black thing. One that secreted an oozing red liquid.

This nightmarish place was also filled with teeming masses of life. Roaming, violent, and monstrous things that towered over her. And up above them all, in the stars that moved and pulsed, larger entities existed as well, nestled in the cosmos.

This was not Hell. It was far beyond that.

This nightmare was now her home, she knew, where she would wait until the Demon of Dunton Farm needed her again.

THE DEMONIC

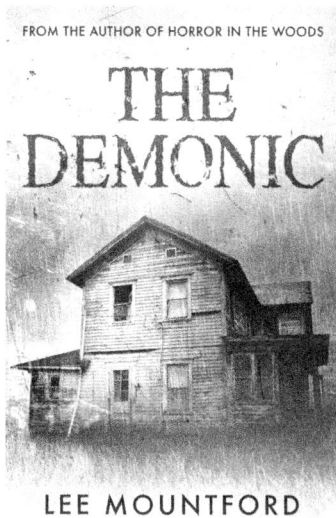

The Demon on the Farm is a prequel story to my second full-length novel, *The Demonic*. So, if you enjoyed this short story, be sure to pick up The Demonic and settle in for a terrifying haunted house novel that will have you on the edge of your seat.

Buy *The Demonic* now.

THE BRASS FARM MURDERS

You may be interested to know that the story of Thomas Kerr, outlined in the last story, is actually based on real-life events that happened in my home town of Ferryhill, in the North East of England.

While I have changed the names involved, the story, I hope, is quite faithful to real life.

It all happened in 1682, on a farm know as Brass Farm—named after the owners: the Brass family. One evening, the parents visited some friends, who were miles away, and left their three children at home.

Alone.

There was a young farm-hand employed on the grounds, one Andrew Mills. He was known to be of below-average intelligence, but was generally considered harmless. On this night, however, the town of Ferryhill was to see a different side of Andrew Mills.

The parents returned home in the early hours of the next morning, only to find their three children slaughtered. Some reports state that Andrew fled the scene, only to be tracked down by authorities, but most say he simply sat outside of the house, waiting for the parents to return home, mumbling about how sorry he was.

His testimony tells of how *something* had visited him in the night: a monstrous entity, he claimed, got inside of his head and demanded that he kill the children. Fearing it was 'The Devil' himself, Andrew took up his axe and chased the three children upstairs to a bedroom. The children locked themselves inside, but Andrew forced his way through the door—breaking the oldest child's arm as he did. Once inside, he set about the two older children with his axe, concentrating his strikes on their heads and upper bodies. He supposedly even cut their throats to stop the screaming.

Andrew then tracked down the youngest girl, someone he considered a friend, and found her hiding under a bed. The girl pleaded with him to spare her life, and that seemed to work at first. Andrew set down the axe and left.

But fate was not kind to the little girl.

Andrew Mills recounted how the demon then appeared to him again, on the landing as he was leaving, telling him: 'Go back, thou hateful wretch, resume thy cursed knife, I long to view more blood, spare not the young one's life.'

And so, Andrew returned. And—as he put it—*dashed her brains out.*

The young man was tried and executed, hung in a gib for all the town to see as he slowly died. His remains were then left in the metal cage as his body began to rot away.

Till his last breath, Andrew maintained that he had been under the influence of a demon (or more precisely, The Devil), who had made him carry out these vile acts.

Whether the Devil played a part or not, what happened to the children that night, and Andrew's testimony, are all true. They really took place.

The only thing that remains of Brass Farm today is the

old corn mill. I've actually been to it myself, and as kids, we used to say that if you ran around the mill anticlockwise, thirteen times, on the stroke of midnight on Halloween, then Andrew Mills would re-appear and reenact his heinous crimes. This time on whoever had called him back.

Not that it ever happened... that I know of.

Even so, it is interesting to see how much inspiration can be found right on one's own doorstep if you just look hard enough.

Even though the names and places have been changed for my story (and the sequel novel, *The Demonic*), this was the story behind the first section of The Demon on the Farm.

As for the character of Margaret Hobbes? I based her loosely on another real-life person. Not someone from my home town this time, but still from my home County. A woman known as The Dark Angel.

Mary-Ann Cotton.

This woman is thought to have poisoned twenty-one people over a twenty-year period. These consisted of lovers, husbands, and also—sickeningly—her own children.

So, not a nice person! Bit of a bitch, really. But again, local legend played a part in the inspiration. Proof that if you look hard enough, inspiration for dark stories are everywhere. Or I just live in a really fucked up area!

As for the demon in the mill? That's all my idea. Though I'm not sure if it is something to really brag about...

- Lee

ALWAYS AND FOREVER

5

The house is always scary at nighttime.

Mum said that monsters and ghosts are all in my imagination, and that there is nothing in the shadows that could hurt me. I would nod and agree with her, maybe even believe her in the daytime, but it's different at night. Especially in our house. Cracks of light from the big moon in the sky would sometimes get in around mum's thick curtains, but for the most part everything is always dark. The house is old, and big, and has always felt empty since Dad had gone. At night, the only thing I can hear is the big ticking clock downstairs. But then, every so often, the house itself will make a sound, like it is moaning, or in pain. Mum said that all old houses make these noises and that it is nothing to be scared of. She said something about the house settling, but to me, it sounds as if someone else is in here with us, making noises and walking around.

I know there is a ghost here. I just know it.

Once in school, my friend Mike told me all about ghosts: that they are what's left of people after they've died, and that some are bad and want to hurt us. He said that they can appear wherever they want, at any time, and get us, and that they look all rotten and horrible. He said they would make noises at night and moan as well, just to try and scare you. Which is why I'm sure we have a ghost in our house, because that is what I hear at night, but Mum won't listen. I just hope it isn't a bad one. I worry that the ghost here is the nasty man who hurt me.

I remember him. He was horrible. And ugly, too. But I hope and pray that the ghost isn't him, or anyone like him.

I hope it's Dad.

Before I go to bed, I always check around the house, just to make sure no one is hiding there in the dark. I need to make sure Mum is safe. Lying in bed is no good, because how can I protect her if I'm just hiding under my covers, listening for the ghost? I'd rather be up, walking around— quietly, so as to not wake Mum—like I'm doing now.

The kitchen downstairs, like the rest of the house, is different at night as well. The plant close to the fridge looks like a big claw reaching out for me, and I keep thinking there is someone hiding in the corners where the shadows are the deepest. As I walk through the house, I never take my eyes off the dark corners, because, if something is going to jump out and get me, as scary as that is, I want to see it first. And the corners are where I think the ghost lives.

The living room has pictures of us—me, Mum, and Dad —on the mantlepiece above the fire. But most are of me. There are a *lot* of me. Some when I'm younger, even a baby, and others when I'm older. The picture where Mum, Dad and I are at the park is my favourite. We are all smiling. I remember that day. Mum told me she loved me 'always and forever.' She used to say that a lot. But looking at these photos makes me sad.

Dad looks so happy in them, and it makes me think that

if the ghost is him, then why doesn't he just come out and say hello? I wouldn't be scared of that, and neither would Mum, because we would get to see him again. And I know he would want to see us. And that's what makes me worry that the ghost isn't Dad. That it's someone else.

And that scares me.

I tip-toe as best I can back upstairs, holding my breath, worried that something might jump out, but careful not to let the floorboards creak and wake Mum. The house is so quiet that any noise I make will sound really loud. As I walk past Mum's bedroom, I hear a faint sound. I can't tell if it's a moan—I think it is—but it definitely came from a person. Either it is Mum, or someone is in there with her. I suddenly feel cold. Is she in danger? I'm scared to go in, but I have to. I can't let anyone hurt her, not like that man hurt me. I won't let it happen.

I can't remember a lot of that night when the man took me, though I'm not sure why. I try sometimes, but I just get flashes of him grabbing and taking me, but then it gets cloudy after that. Mum's door is already open a little, so I clench my teeth and pop my head in.

No one is in the room with her. It is just Mum, all alone, sitting on her bed, crying quietly. She is looking at a photo. She doesn't see me, but I feel really sad and don't know whether to go over and hug her or leave her alone. I think she is thinking of Dad. That always makes her cry.

'It's okay, Mum,' I tell her, but she doesn't hear me. I know she is upset, but I'm still here for her, so why does she always ignore me? All I want is to protect her.

It seems like such a long time since we've spoken to each other.

I walk over and sit on the bed next to her and put my arm round her. She stops crying for a moment and looks up, like my dog Benji used to do when he heard something outside. But Mum looks only for a moment. Then she goes back to looking at the picture of Dad. Only, when I look at it, I realise the picture isn't of Dad.

It's of me.

'It's okay, Mum, don't be sad I'm right here.'

She still ignores me.

'She can't hear you, son.'

I look up to the door of Mum's room and see him, standing there, looking exactly like I remember. My legs feel weak, hollow. I can't believe it.

Dad is here.

'Dad!' I shout. 'Mum, look, it's Dad!' Still, I get nothing from her. 'What's wrong with her?' I ask him.

'She can't see you, son. Or hear you. She doesn't know you're there,' he tells me. He is looking at me the same way he looked when he told me Benji died.

'But why?' I ask, and then another question jumps out of my mouth, almost as quickly as it jumped into my head. 'Dad, how come you're here? I thought that you…' I trail off, unsure how to finish what I was saying.

'I did, son,' he says. 'I never wanted to leave you and Mum, but it was just my time.'

'So, now you've come back?'

He doesn't answer straight away, and I see his eyes get wet. He holds out his arms to me like he used to do when he wanted a hug. I look back to Mum, who still doesn't seem to know we are there, then run over to him. He hugs me so tightly, and I hug him right back.

'Son,' he says, kneeling down so that we are face to face. 'What I'm going to tell you will be a little confusing, but I need you to trust me. And don't be scared.'

'Okay,' I tell him. 'I won't be scared. I'm brave.'

'I know you are. You know when I told you I had to go away, because it was my time? Remember, when I was sick?'

'Yes,' I say with a nod. He looks a lot better than the last time I saw him. He looks stronger. Not so thin. 'I remember, Dad.'

He is quiet for a long time. Then he gives me a smile, but a sad one. 'Well, it's your time too, son.'

I don't understand. Not at first. Then I feel a little sick as it starts to make sense.

'You mean?'

He nods quickly, almost like he doesn't want me to finish what I was going to say. Which is good, because I don't want to say it.

Instead, I decide to ask him how it happened, and when. But then—all of a sudden—I just know. It makes sense.

'The man who took me?' I ask, and he nods again. He looks angry, and tears run down his face. I hug him, and we stay that way for a long time. Eventually, he pulls away, cupping my face with his hands. Though I can't remember exactly when it happened, I know the man had taken me sometime after Dad had died, because Dad wasn't here to protect me.

'It's time to go, son.'

'But what about Mum?' I ask and look back to her. She seems so sad, so hurt. I don't want to go without her.

'She has to stay here.'

'We can't leave her!'

'I'm sorry, but there is no other way. You'll see her again, one day.'

As he says that, I notice a light creep in from under the door and through the curtains. It is white and quickly gets brighter and brighter, so bright that it starts to hurt my eyes.

'What's that?' I ask.

'That means it's time,' he says. 'I need to take you back.'

'Back where?'

'Don't worry, son, its safe there,' Dad says, and takes my hand. 'Hold on to me and we'll go back together.'

The light gets brighter and brighter. It feels nice against my face—like the warm sun—but I don't want to leave Mum, not all on her own like this. It isn't fair.

'I don't want to go,' I say, but my voice sounds like an echo.

'You need to come with me. Try not to be scared.'

His voice is all echoey now as well. I think I know where we are supposed to go now. I'm not scared. But I don't want to leave Mum all on her own.

'No,' I say, and struggle to get free. He tightens his grip.

'This is important, son. Just stay with me. It's okay.'

The light becomes brighter and brighter, and my body starts to feel strange. It gets lighter, somehow, and I feel like I could float away. It's actually nice. The light then gets so bright that I can't see anymore.

'No,' I yell again, and yank my hand free. Then, as quickly as I can blink, the light is gone.

And so is Dad.

Everything around me is dark again. And it is quiet, apart from Mum, who is still crying quietly. She shouldn't cry, though, because whether she knows it or not, I'll be here to protect her.

Always and forever.

LET ME THROUGH

6-1

To: CRichards@pixiedesign.com
   From: Peter.Richards@demoserve.com
   Subject: Home

Hi Babe,

I'll be home as expected tomorrow morning. Can't wait to see you and Alfie. Bit of a weird one this job, so will be glad to see the back of it. Flying out tonight, so can hopefully sleep a little on the plane. I've missed you both so much. I know it's only been a couple of weeks, but it feels longer. I didn't like that place. Even Troy said it had a bad vibe.

Anyway, I'm rambling here. I'll see you both tomorrow! And I've decided to push my other contracts back a bit. We're in a good position and I've earned some time off.

Love you,

Pete

~

To: Peter.Richards@demoserve.com
From: CRichards@pixiedesign.com
Subject: Re: Home

That is so great! I keep telling you to take time off. Glad that I've finally got through to you, lol.

Sounds like this job was a bit of a bad one? Still, it's finished now. And you can look forward to coming home to me and Alfie, where you belong. The bed is here waiting for you, and I'm going to be waiting in it ;)

Hopefully that will keep your spirits up!

Can't wait for you to get home, hun. Safe flight and see you tomorrow.

Cassie x

～

To: CRichards@pixiedesign.com
From: Peter.Richards@demoserve.com
Subject: Re: Home

Oh, that *is* keeping my spirits up alright. When I get back I'm gonna throw you on that bed and fuck you so hard you won't be able to walk for a week.

～

To: CRichards@pixiedesign.com
From: Peter.Richards@demoserve.com
Subject: Re: Home

Jesus Christ, I'm so sorry, babe! I don't know what the hell came over me. I've never been good at dirty talk. But that was a bit much. Really sorry. I must be tired.

X

~

To: Peter.Richards@demoserve.com
From: CRichards@pixiedesign.com
Subject: Re: Home

Wow! I was gonna say, lol. You've never spoken like that before, haha. It's no problem, hun. Try and rest on the flight and I'll see you tomorrow.

This little boy, sleeping in my arms, is perfect.

He is only six months old, and I just cannot imagine anything more perfect. God, just looking at his little pudgy face makes my heart want to burst with joy. I know that sometimes mothers have difficulty bonding with a new baby, and I thank my lucky stars that Alfie and I did not have that problem.

Both he and Pete are my everything.

Alfie has deep blue eyes, like his father, but he gets his dark hair from me. Some people say he looks like me, others that he looks like Peter, but I think people just see what they want to see. To me, he just looks like... perfection.

I lay him carefully down in his crib but don't bother to set the automated mobile dangling above. It plays a lovely lullaby that he likes, but with Alfie in such a deep sleep already, there isn't much point. I look down on him, and he rolls himself over to be face down—his preferred sleeping position. I giggle as he lifts his bum in the air and tucks his legs under his belly, all snuggled in. How he can sleep like this, I have no idea, but he does. And he makes a cute little sigh, content in his slumber.

But, as much as he fills me with joy, he also fills me with worry. He's so small, dependent, and vulnerable. The thought of failing and something bad happening to this little thing is a terrifying—and ever present—worry. And whenever such notions start to creep into my mind, I'm always quick to bat them away, not daring to let myself think them through. Because even the initial idea that springs up is terrifying enough to make my heart seize.

Alfie is our first, and though I dearly hope we will have more, looking after him often feels like a wing and a prayer. Like the two of us—Pete and I—have no idea what we are doing, or how to be responsible for this little life. I doubt myself constantly, and feel that at some point I will do something seriously wrong and that Alfie will get hurt or become sick or worse... *No! Stop thinking like that!*

Alfie is generally a happy baby. And, as Pete always says, surely that is a sign we are doing something right.

I check my watch and see that Pete should be home soon. Any time now. He already called to say his flight had landed, so now he is travelling back from the airport.

He sounded exhausted. And somehow... off. As if something was playing on his mind. I just hope things aren't getting on top of him again. He tends to get distant when that happens, and I don't want things to get too bad again. He's come too far, given me too much. He deserves to be happy and to leave that darkness behind.

However, I know that he can never totally extinguish the darkness that plagues him. It is part of him, much as he doesn't want it to be. A constant, throbbing, and unrelenting black wave that rises and crashes with varying levels of intensity. That was how he once described his depression to me. Sometimes the flow of the black—that is what he calls it —can be shallow. Those times are easier, even though he can still feel that trickle run through him. Other times, the waves are too big, too overwhelming, and they can swallow him up.

I just wonder if that email from him last night is a sign of things getting worse. Pete has never said anything so filthy to me. Not that I mind, to be honest, but in his own words, he struggles with things like that. It just isn't him. So, coming from Pete, they just seemed wrong. Like they had come from someone else.

Shyness is a part of Pete, too. In some ways he is so confident, but in others... not so much. Which is crazy, because he really doesn't seem to know how attractive he is, dwelling on smaller things like his growing belly—which isn't as bad as he thinks it is.

And his scars.

My thoughts are broken as I hear the front door open. I smile, check the baby camera is switched on and pointing at Alfie, and quietly make my way downstairs.

Pete is standing at the front door. My blue-eyed boy. Light brown hair, scruffy but stylish. Same with the stubble on his strong jaw. Pete is a tall man, and while not quite stocky, he certainly isn't thin, which I like. I even adore his belly, though he hates it so.

At the sight of him, my heart fills with joy again. Pete used to be the only person that could do that to me, until Alfie came along. But I know he doesn't mind sharing that honour now.

I run to him and throw my arms around his neck and jump into his arms. We kiss. I pull back and we smile at each other.

'I missed you,' I say.

'And I missed you, too,' Pete replies. The smile on his lips is wide, but it doesn't reach his eyes.

Something is wrong. The black is there again. Just behind the happy facade. It took me a while to learn to read him, but I can always spot it now.

I stay strong and kiss him again. As dark as things can get for him, I will always be his guiding light, shining the way to happiness. To me and Alfie.

Hold on to me, baby, I think. *Things are going to be alright. In fact, they are going to be perfect.*

Because there is nothing in this world that can ruin what we have.

After a great day together, with Pete spending a lot of time bonding with Alfie, we finally put the little boy down for the night and have a little 'us' time. I prepared a meal of spaghetti bolognese—Pete's favourite—which he hungrily devoured, and we settled on the sofa with a glass of red wine each.

'So, what was it about the job that you didn't like?' I ask him.

'Well, I've never worked on a church before,' he replies before taking a large mouthful from his glass. He swallows and goes on, 'I thought I would love it. And, at first, I did. Though it seemed wrong to be demolishing a place like that, even if it was only a small section. But it was still a great chance to work in a place that was different to what I normally do.'

'And overseas as well,' I say. 'You've not travelled that far before.'

'I know.'

'So what was it that you didn't like? Sounds great so far.'

'At first, it *was* great. Kind of what I thought it would be.

But after a few days, the place started to feel... weird. Like I wasn't alone there.'

'You weren't. Troy was with you. And surely there would have been others working through the renovation, too?'

'Yeah, but that's not what I mean. I always felt like...' he trails off and averts eye contact, his cheeks flushing a little.

I put a hand on his knee. 'It's okay, you can tell me. I won't judge. You know that.'

'Well, it kind of felt like I was always being watched by something I couldn't see. And it felt oppressive as hell. The air itself just seemed... heavy. I don't know how else to describe it.'

'Sounds freaky.'

'You must think I'm nuts.'

I laugh. '*Me* think you're nuts? I'm the one who believes in stuff like that. *You* always said *I* was nuts.'

Pete holds his hands up and laughed. 'I'm not saying I believe in it, or that it was a ghost or any of that,' he says. 'It was just... weird. I didn't like it. And there was...' Again he trails off, and again he doesn't make eye contact.

'What?' I push, dearly wanting to know.

'Nothing,' he says.

'No, tell me. It's okay, you can tell me anything.'

'I'm tired of talking,' he says and sets his wine glass down on the side table. Then he takes mine and sets it down as well. I notice a hungry look in his eyes. 'I want to do something else.'

'And what's that?' I ask with a smile. Pete answers by leaning forward and kissing me. A strong, passionate kiss, and then he moves further forward still, pushing me down into the sofa and climbing atop me. It's a welcome surprise, as often I tend to be the initiator in things like this. I almost ask if he is going to make good on the promise from his email, to rib him gently, but don't want to risk putting him off of his stride or making him self-conscious. Instead, I let his hands run all over me, settling on my breasts, grabbing them firmly. The hard squeeze on my left nipple causes a jolt of pain, that both makes me gasp and helps to excite me.

'Should we go upstairs?' I ask him.

He shakes his head. 'I don't want to wait.'

So we don't. Instead, he pulls me down to the floor where there is more room, allowing us to stretch out a little. His tongue again finds its way into my mouth, even more forcefully this time, and I feel my eyes go wide as I nearly gag.

'Go a little more steady,' I say after pulling away. But he is too excited by what he is doing, and I can feel his hardness pressing into my stomach through his jeans as he lies on top of me. I'm not even sure he heard my slight protest, which worries me a little, making me feel more an object to be used rather than a participant in what is about to happen. It is not something I've ever felt with Pete before.

Then, a hand finds its way around my throat and squeezes. Not too hard, but enough to startle me. Part of me likes it, finds it exciting, but the other side of me is worried at how he is acting. I push his chest upwards, forcing his lips from mine, and make firm eye contact.

'Slow down!' I order. 'You're being too rough.'

At first he looks annoyed at the disruption, but then he seems to gain focus and looks down at his hand, the one gripping my neck. His eyes go wide.

'I'm so sorry,' he says, rolling off me quickly. He sits upright and puts his head in his hands. 'I don't know what came over me.' He then turns to look at me, his face a picture of concern. 'Are you okay?'

'I'm fine,' I say with as big a smile as I can muster. 'You

just got a little carried away, is all. Understandable, considering we haven't seen each other for weeks.'

'But... I mean... I had my hand...'

'It's okay,' I tell him, rubbing his back. 'Just take it a little slower.'

I lean into him this time, and we kiss again. He is reluctant, so I push him back down to the floor, and this time I climb on top of him.

'Are you sure?' he asks. I can see shame in his expression.

'I'm sure,' I say. 'I'm pretty sturdy. Don't worry about it.'

I kiss him again and unbutton his jeans. Wiggling my hand inside, I take hold of him, but find that his hardness is gone. He is limp in my hand. I stroke at it and kiss him, nibble his earlobe, and then lightly pull at his hair.

Nothing.

I have a sinking feeling that Pete has disappeared inside of his head and that he and penis are no longer on the same wavelength. The disconnect is there. I keep trying, but when I catch his eye, I can see that look of shame has only deepened. His mind is no longer on arousal or pleasure, but guilt and worry.

Not the homecoming present I would have wanted, but it is what it is.

'It's fine,' I tell him.

He shakes his head and looks away.

'Is everything okay?' I ask. I don't show it, but I'm worried that something is very wrong. I'm worried the dark waves are growing again. I put my hand on his chest. 'You can talk to me, you know.' I pause, then add, 'Let me through.'

He looks at me. I've used that phrase before with him. A few times. When I'm worried about him, it has become a kind of signal from me, to tell him—without saying the exact words—that I'm concerned he's slipping. Pete then turns his eyes away.

'I'm sorry. I don't know what the fuck is wrong with me,' he says.

'Nothing is wrong with you,' I tell him. 'It's no big deal. So don't make it one, hun.' I cup his chin and kiss him gently. We could leave things a while and try again, that sometimes works, but his reaction upon realising he was being so overzealous tells me that he is too far removed to get excited now. His dick's lack of participation isn't new to us, but it hasn't happened in a long while.

'Come on,' I say, and stand up, offering him my hand. 'Let's just go to bed and snuggle. You can hold me and we can fall asleep together. Don't let any of this get into your head. We have lots of time to spend together, so we don't have to rush anything.'

While his eyes still look sad, a slight smile crosses his lips. It seems genuine. Almost grateful for my understanding. He takes my hand and gets to his feet.

'Sorry,' he says again. Before I can scold him for apologising too much, he puts a finger to my lips. 'But thank you.' Then, looking into my eyes, he adds, 'I love you, Cass, more than anything.'

'I love you, too,' I tell him, then smile. 'But there is someone upstairs who may take issue with what you just said.'

He laughs. 'Okay, more than *nearly* anything. Alfie has a good claim, too.'

I kiss him again and we go up to bed. I fall asleep in his arms, feeling safe in his embrace, but with a sinking feeling in my gut.

6-4

I wake.

In the darkness of night, my eyes take a moment to adjust.

Just after Alfie was born, I went through a phase of not sleeping very well, waking many times during the night, feeling panicked—scared that something had happened to him or that he needed my help. As the weeks went by, that fear seemed to fade. That, or my body became used to it. And, as Alfie started to sleep through, so did I. Broken sleep became infrequent.

So, I have no idea what it is that has woken me now. All is silent, so I don't think a noise has disturbed me. I try to think of what I was dreaming about, considering that maybe a bad dream that has disturbed me, but I can remember nothing.

And yet, I feel tense.

I roll to my side, instinctively checking the clock, as well as the baby monitor on my nightstand. The digital clock tells me it is just after three in the morning. The monitor, which relays sound as well as video, shows a display from the camera set in Alfie's room. One that is mounted on a high shelf, looking down on him. The low-res image on the small monitor has a light blue hue to it—due to the night vision that is activated on the camera. It is clear enough to see my beautiful son, who lies on his front with his legs tucked up and bum in the air. He seems peaceful. Content. Though I have to squint to see it, I can just make out the gentle rise and fall of his back as he breathes. From what I can see, all seems well.

Almost.

At the side of the image, just creeping into shot, I see movement—the edge of something swaying into the frame before quickly drifting back out. I quickly sit up in the bed and panic fills me.

I turn to wake Pete, ready to pull him out of bed with me to run and check on our child, but he is not there. The covers on his side have been pulled back, and I can see the crumpled under-sheets from where he was lying.

'Pete?' I call out in a loud whisper. No response. But I can't wait. I have no idea what it was that I'd seen on the monitor, so I need to check. Concern for my own well-being is quickly and easily pushed aside, overwhelmed by the fear of what might happen to my son. I am quickly on my feet, and I run out to the landing, stopping to see the door to Alfie's room is wide open.

Through it, I can see Pete. He is standing close to the baby's crib. Not quite motionless, as he is swaying gently. I know immediately that it was Pete I saw drift into view on the monitor. Probably the top of his head, from where he was standing.

But what the hell is he doing?

'Pete?' I whisper again. Still no answer. I make my way over to him, creeping into the room and squeezing past my husband, listening to the light and steady snore from the baby. Pete's face is titled down as he stands stock-still, save for the gentle sway. His eyes are closed. It's like he is watching Alfie without actually looking at him.

I feel pinpricks run up my back. Pete has never, as far as I'm aware, had a problem with sleepwalking. Yet here he is, obviously asleep, and standing over our child.

I put an arm on his shoulder—as gently as I can—hoping not to startle him, so that I can gently guide him back to bed. He doesn't seem to feel or notice my touch. I try to move him away, but he will not budge, his body so rigid and firm it is like pulling against a statue.

'Pete,' I say again, my voice soft and light, so as not to disturb Alfie. Again, no response. At first. I see him give a small shake of his head, and for the first time, I then notice a film of sweat on his forehead. He starts to whisper something. I think he is responding to me, initially, but the shaking of his head becomes more vigorous, and the single word he utters, over and over, becomes more frantic.

'No. No, no, no.'

I am about to speak, when he adds, 'I won't. I won't. No.'

He sounds scared. God knows who he is responding to in whatever dream he is having, but he is clearly afraid of them.

He becomes louder, and, as much as I know that you aren't supposed to wake someone who is sleepwalking, I don't want him to wake Alfie. So, I grab his arm and pull, ready to try and catch Pete if he falls. He stumbles a few steps, then his eyes snap wide open. I keep hold of his arm, stroking it, making soothing shushing sounds. He looks disoriented and panicked, which is only natural, I suppose. His eyes flit about wildly, until he eventually notices me.

'It's okay,' I whisper, and continue to rub his arm. I then

put a hand around the back of his neck and pull him closer into a hug. I can hear his rapid, shallow breaths. 'Calm down.'

'Where... where am I?'

I don't need to answer, as I see realisation draw over him. After that, he starts to slowly relax. 'Come,' I whisper. 'Let's go back to bed.'

'I don't remember...'

'You were sleepwalking.'

'Sleepwalking?'

I feel the tension in his body ease a little.

'Come on,' I say, 'before we wake Alfie.'

I lead Pete back to the bedroom—he comes willingly now—and into bed. 'That's so weird,' he says. 'Never happened before.'

I push him back so he lies down. 'Tell me about it,' I say. 'It was freaky to see. Do you remember what you were dreaming about? You seemed upset.'

With his head on the pillow, Pete turns to me, his brow furrowed. 'I can't remember. Feels like something bad. I can still feel my heart going. But the more I try to remember, the more it slips from my mind.'

'Don't worry about it,' I tell him and press a hand to his chest. 'Just go back to sleep.'

'I guess,' he says. 'Sorry for scaring you.'

'You didn't scare me,' I say, which isn't totally true. The sight of him like that, standing over Alfie, did unnerve me a little. 'But if you had woken our baby, you know you'd have had hell to pay.'

'I can believe it,' he says with a tired smile, and I snuggle into him, as I had before we fell asleep. It takes Pete less than half an hour to drift off again, and I can tell by the rise and fall of his chest, in time with his deep breathing, that he's gone. I can't fall asleep as quickly, however. I keep thinking of what Pete was saying while sleepwalking.

No. No. No. No. I won't. I won't.

It sounded like he was talking to someone unseen. I know in my head it was just part of his dreaming, but something about it has spooked me.

It's all in your head, I tell myself. But the ominous feeling I've had since Pete's returned is only starting to grow.

6-5

Today has been a good day.

The sun shone brightly and we spent most of the morning and early afternoon at the park, as a family, idling around. A picnic dinner, Pete playing with Alfie on the blanket on the grass, and smiles all round. It was such a good day that the uneasy feeling that had been growing in me has completely subsided during our time out of the house together. And, after a quiet start, Pete is also different today. He seems happier, with no worries, nothing weighing him down. It was a day full of laughter.

And it was much needed.

But things are a little different now. Alfie is in bed, asleep, and Pete is on top of me, thrusting away. His face is a picture of aggressive pleasure. His hand is round my throat again. I want to stop him. To tell him no. But at the same time, I don't want the same thing to happen that did the previous night—I don't want to make him feel low and useless. I put my hand on the scar that covers the left side of his chest and shoulder, the burn mark from his youth. Usually, even the slightest touch here is enough to make him jolt a little. Not through pain—he just hates if I touch it, ashamed of the unsightly mess and what it represents. Only in his mind, of course, but it is enough for him to normally shrink back from my touch.

At the moment, however, he doesn't even notice.

In truth, if it weren't for my worry over this sudden change in sexual attitude, this dominance and assertiveness would be quite welcome, and quite a turn-on.

But no. This is too much of a change. Too different. He speeds up, but I decide to tell him to stop. I need to know what is going on with him. As I'm about to speak, he spasms and lets out a sound I haven't heard from him before. This isn't his normal groan of release. It is a growl. I feel him spill his orgasm inside of me.

Then he collapses to my side, panting heavily. He says nothing. In that moment, I don't feel like his wife, his lover, or his soul mate. I feel like a means to an end. Something to use and then discard. I pull the sheets up to my chin. It isn't cold, but I suddenly feel like it is. And I wait for him to talk to me. To say something about what just happened. But, instead, I soon hear his snores.

That gnawing in my gut that was gone—or ignored—for much of the day has now returned. Something is clearly not right with Pete. And I want to help him. To be his guiding light through the darkness that is part of him. But, somehow, this feels different. Never, even in his darkest moments, has Pete ever treated me as anything less than someone who deserves love and respect. Much less a mere object for his fulfilment. His illness has never previously involved reducing me.

I know it's true that, if there are millions of people who are unfortunate enough to suffer from depression, then there are millions of different conditions and symptoms, all summed up in that one word, which isn't really enough. But actions like what I have just endured have never been the results of Pete's symptoms.

Perhaps it is a sign that things are getting worse? And that something bad is coming with his condition?

But that just didn't feel right to me. I am certain that this was somehow different.

I cry, quietly. Not sobbing—but my eyes ran. I am scared. Scared for us—for our family—and for our future.

Or perhaps this is all in my head.

Am I just making a huge problem where none exists? If I had just spoken up, then there wouldn't have been an issue. I am ovulating, too, and even though the chances are against us getting pregnant with a one-off like that, I am still worried. I don't want our next child conceived under such circumstances. Which is in itself foolish, I guess. What difference does that make? Pete and I will get past this small hump—we always did—and go on being happy despite it all. We haven't officially said we are trying, but then, we didn't say that with Alfie, either.

I roll to my side, casting my gaze at the baby monitor, looking at Alfie's sleeping form. So peaceful. So perfect. I close my eyes and hope sleep will come quickly, so that I can forget tonight and move on afresh tomorrow.

Then I hear it.

A crackled sound comes through the monitor. My eyes snap open. Alfie is still unmoving in his crib and at first I think that perhaps he let out a moan in his sleep. But that doesn't fit. The sound I heard was more like a distant voice, saying something that was totally incomprehensible to me, yet distinct and intentional. And it was spoken in a distorted whisper.

As I doubt myself, I hear it again.

'*Per me.*'

Then I see something shift on the monitor: a shadow cast over the light blue image of my son. How that is possible in a room without a light source, I do not know. But it is unmistakable.

My blood runs cold.

I jump out of bed and run from my room, then down the landing, bursting into Alfie's room and bracing to find something. What, I have no idea. An intruder perhaps, who has snuck in during the night. Some sick fuck who for some reason has targeted my son.

But, as I shoulder charge the door open and flick on the light, I am met with a room that—other than Alfie—is completely empty. My heart pounds in my chest, and I look frantically around the room: under the crib, in Alfie's wardrobe, behind the curtains. But there is nothing.

No one.

Alife starts to groan and roll over, his sleep disturbed. He then starts to cry. I know I that should switch off his light and then pick him up to nurse him back to sleep, but I can't. I still am not certain his room is as clear as it seems. I can almost feel something else in here. Alfie's crying rises in volume. Eventually my heart begins to slow, but his cries wake Pete, who stumbles into the room, still half asleep.

'Everything okay?' he asks, his voice groggy.

I pick up the baby and snuggle him into me. 'Fine,' I lie. 'Alfie just woke up, so I'm going to get him back off.' Another lie.

'Want me to help?'

'It's okay, I've got this. Just go back to bed.'

He nods, smiles, then turns and stumbles from the room. I rock Alfie in my arms and flick off the bedroom light. The sudden darkness feels heavy and oppressive. Almost like it has a physical weight to it.

There is clearly no one here with us, but I know what I saw on that monitor. And what I heard.

Per me.

Spoken in a voice that didn't seem natural. And with an inflection that indicated the words were not English, though I don't know what language they actually were.

I am eventually able to get Alfie back off to sleep. I just hope his night's rest has not been too badly broken already. I set him back down again and look around the room once more, my eyes straining in the darkness.

I can see nothing.

Was it all in my head? Could the words spoken just have been Alfie's murmurs—something my tired mind took and made into something else? And the shadow, just a distortion from the low-quality camera or a flickering of the pixels?

I don't know what to think, but I know I can't stand here all night.

After a few more moments, I go back to the master bedroom feeling slightly foolish. But I leave the doors to both Alfie's room and the master bedroom open. Just in case.

Sleep does not come easily.

6-6

How the hell am I supposed to bring up last night when today Pete seems so oblivious to his actions?

We went out of the house again—Pete's idea—to a local coffee shop in town for dinner. It is a quaint and quiet place that I frequent when I can. It's small, but big enough for the amount of clientele it gets. We are the only ones in, other than two members of staff behind the counter. The walls are clad with dark timber panels at the base, then deliberately antiquated wallpaper above: a dull pastel green with gold-embossed flower patterns.

I finish my sandwich and start to pick at the cupcake on the table before me. Pete guzzles down the last of his coffee, smacking his lips together as he finishes.

'I could go for another,' he says. 'Want a refill?'

I shake my head and then Pete gets up to order another coffee. Alfie is in his pram next to me, asleep again after his feed. I decide that I need to stop messing around and speak to Pete. Whatever is going on will only get worse if it remains in the shadows. Pretending to ignore something like this only lets it fester and grow, like a mold in the dark that is left unchecked.

And it appears that it was affecting me more than I first thought—seeing and hearing things in the night and rushing into Alfie's room over what turned out to be nothing; paranoia is not something I enjoy dealing with.

Pete comes back, steaming mug of coffee in hand that smells delicious. Mine is growing cold and sits unfinished, but even so I now regret not asking for another. Perhaps after we've cleared the air.

Doing that always makes me feel better.

'I need to talk to you about something,' I say.

He holds my eye contact, looking a little worried. Then he reaches over and puts a hand on mine. He can see the seriousness in my expression and is clearly worried. Not for himself, I can tell, but for me. This is the Pete I know and love. Which makes it all the more difficult to understand how he could have treated me the way he did last night—so coldly, like an object.

'Do you remember last night?' I ask.

He nods. 'Of course.'

'And you remember us being... intimate?'

He pauses and frowns a little. Not an angry frown, more a one of concentration as he searches his memory. 'I guess,' he says, sounding a little confused. 'But only a little. Didn't we just have sex then go to sleep?'

'Kind of,' I say. 'At least, you did.'

'I don't follow.'

'Do you remember much about it? The sex, I mean?'

His mouth opens a little, then he pauses. He drops back in his seat. 'I... I honestly can't.' He looks worried now. 'Why can't I remember it?'

'You were pretty rough,' I tell him, gently.

His eyes go wide. 'I'm so sorry,' he says, but I can tell that he really doesn't know what he's apologising for. Not because he doesn't think he's done anything wrong, but because he really can't remember it. He is just taking my word that something has happened.

'You really can't remember, can you?' I ask, but it is more of a confirmative statement than a question.

'I can't. I honestly can't.'

This is new. Was he so lost in passion that he wasn't really in control? And was it just passion, or was there something more to it?

I stroke his hand. 'It's okay,' I tell him. The statement is both true and false. It is fine and it isn't. 'And after you finished, you just rolled over and went to sleep. I felt a little used.'

His cheeks flush a deep red that is exacerbated by the pallor that comes to the rest of his face.

'Oh, hun, I'm so sorry.'

Sorry.

It is a word he's used a lot. More so in the last few days. I have no doubt that he meant it each and every time, but it is that he keeps needing to use it that is troubling.

He goes on. 'I don't know what the hell is up with me. I can barely remember having sex.' His voice grows a little too loud to be comfortable, and I worry the nearby staff might hear what should be a private conversation.

'It's okay,' I tell him again. Something I realise that I have been saying more and more often. And, again, it isn't completely truthful. I lean forward in my seat. 'But I need you to talk to me. Things seem different since you got back. You don't seem yourself. It's like you are slipping again. And we agreed that if you ever felt that way, you would talk to me. So, I need you to talk to me.'

He is silent, searching for the words. The confused frown only deepens. 'I... I didn't even realise I was,' he says, sounding earnest. 'But I guess you're right.'

'So how are you feeling? Are things getting overwhelming again?'

He shakes his head. 'I... I don't know. I don't think so.'

'Come on,' I encourage. 'Please, talk. Let me through. I can't be your guiding light if you don't let me.'

'I'm being honest,' he replies. 'It doesn't feel like it normally does. I feel heavy, I suppose. Like there is a weight on top of me. But it's different. It seems more... external. Though I know that doesn't make sense.'

'It doesn't have to make sense,' I tell him. 'If that's how you feel, I want to hear it.'

And it's true—what he told me *doesn't* have to make sense. Not at all. Nothing about the depression he is suffering through makes sense. That's what makes it so maddening for him. He once described it as trying to fix something that was incomprehensible to him. An impossible task. And it got so bad, only a few years ago, that he even made an attempt on his own life. Something I will never let happen again.

'And nothing happened on the trip to trigger it?' I ask. Sometimes there are triggers to these things. Other times not.

He shakes his head. 'I don't think so.' As he says it, I can tell something popped into his mind. A memory perhaps. I can see it weigh on him, and his eyes narrow as his expression drops a little.

'What is it?' I ask, pushing further. I need to hear this. 'Please tell me. Let me through, hun,' I urge.

'Just, the thing last night. The fact I can't really remember. Something similar happened on that trip.'

I lean forward. My first thought is a stupid one: that he forced himself on someone else. But I quickly realise that is not what he means at all, and I feel ashamed for thinking it. 'A memory lapse?' I ask, realising what he meant.

He nods. 'Yeah. Towards the end. The last day. There are a couple of hours I just can't place.'

The gnawing in my gut deepens. That's another symptom that is completely new.

'And this kind of thing has never happened before?' I ask, just to make sure, thinking perhaps it was a symptom he suffered before I knew him.

But Pete shakes his head, confirming my suspicion. 'Never.'

'Okay,' I say, taking a breath. 'But we know something is happening. It's out there now. Not bottled up inside of you. So, we can do something.'

'But what?' he asks, looking concerned.

'We can make an appointment to see Dr. Caryll again. Talk it through with him. See what he says. Perhaps it means medication again, perhaps not. But let's just take this first step. What do you say?'

He is quiet for a moment, but then he looks to Alfie. He nods. 'Yeah,' he agrees. 'We'll do that.' Then he looks back to me. 'But I'm worried, Cass. Somehow, this just feels... different.'

I feel a little better after the talk with Pete earlier today.

We have booked an appointment to see Dr. Caryll for next week. Pete called on his mobile and set it up as soon as we left the coffee shop. Which means he isn't at the stage where he starts to let things just wash over him and ignore them. He still has agency.

The appointment will not be a fix to what is happening, of course. At least not completely. There is no magic pill to fix all of this. And life just doesn't work that way, anyway. I know that. Long ago I learned that life is just a series of ups and downs and problems and hassles and laughing and crying and sun and rain. It is never a fixed state. Not all problems have quick solutions. Some don't have solutions at all, only ways to manage them. But that manageability makes everything worth it.

And Pete is more than worth it. He is everything to me. He and Alfie. Everyone has their baggage—I'm damn sure I do—but with Pete that is insignificant compared to the good times we have and the joy and love we bring to each other.

And because of that, when all is said and done, I am still extremely lucky. So I am damn sure I am going to keep fighting for Pete and do whatever I can to help him get better.

Which was the excuse I gave myself to tap out an email on my phone when Pete nipped to the toilet. I addressed it to Travis, Pete's some-time work colleague.

Travis has his own business, as Pete does, but the two companies complement each other and often work on larger projects together. It helps that Pete and Travis are good friends, too.

The trip abroad had been one such project. Perhaps Travis could offer a little more insight into what had happened out there. Peter will perhaps tell all he can, if I push him, but by his own admission, there are gaps in his memory. Gaps that Travis may be able to fill in.

The email was quick and to the point:

∼

Hey Travis, it's Cass. I'm just emailing about Pete. Please don't discuss this with him, but he hasn't quite been himself since coming back. I feel a bit stupid asking, but did anything happen out there that I should know about? Something that could explain things? Let me know.

Cass

∼

I hover my finger over the 'send' button. Am I going behind Pete's back with this? How would he feel if he found out? And is my need to help—or at least, help as I see it—actually breaking Pete's trust? The more I think about it, the more I realise it is the wrong thing to do. I was stupid to even think it. With my thumb close to the button, I decide against sending it.

I hear the flush of the toilet upstairs and, perhaps because I've been lost in my thoughts, the sudden sound startles me... and my thumb twitches.

It hits the send button, and a sinking feeling of betrayal draws over me.

Fuck. Fuck. Fuck.

I try to think of a way to cancel what I've done, but a ping quickly sounds from my phone. *Email successfully sent.*

Fuck. Fuck. Fuck.

Is there a way to recall it? I have no idea. I open my web browser to search for a way, but Pete soon emerges, and I have to quickly put my phone away. He walks up to me and gives me a kiss on the cheek, before sitting down on the play-mat with Alfie, who is shaking a rattle and giggling to himself. Pete smiles, then looks up to me.

'Thank you for earlier,' he says. 'It means a lot. I don't know what I'd do without you. I'll get through this, Cass. I promise.'

Tears bubble up in me, and I bend down and hug him. 'I know you will,' I say, feeling terrible at what I've done. I pull back and look him in the eyes. I have to tell him. But Pete smiles and kisses me again.

'Come on,' he says. 'Let's play with Alfie. These moments will be gone before we know it.' He grabs a different rattling toy, which he shakes above his son. The noise draws the blue-eyed boy's attention, and he giggles again.

I try to join in, but feel absolutely terrible. I have betrayed Pete when all he needs is support.

It makes me feel worse about ten minutes later when I

feel a vibration from the phone in my pocket and hear the audio cue of an arriving email ring out. While it could be an email from anyone, somehow I know who it is.

Travis has sent a reply.

'An email?' Pete asks. Like him, I have different sound alerts for the different message types received on my phone, and he has grown used to them and knows which is which. I am the same with him, and the *ping* from his emails are a constant source of irritation to me, given how constant they are for his business.

'I guess,' I reply.

'You not checking it?'

'It can wait. Probably spam,' I lie, and we continue to play with Alfie. But as much as I try to ignore it, and as bad as I felt for sending the message to Travis in the first place, part of me dearly wants to read this reply.

And I get my chance. After a few hours of play, and after feeding Alfie, he grows tired, and Pete goes up to put the little boy down for his nap. As soon as Pete is out of the room, I retrieve my phone and see that it was indeed a reply from Travis:

~

Hi Cass, good to hear from you. And yeah, hasn't Pete told you? There were a few hours there where... I don't really know how to put this. Well, we just couldn't find him. Anywhere. He was missing. I panicked like fuck, in all honesty. Then he turned up again. Looked a little woozy. Spaced out. Not quite himself. But he soon pulled around. Said he couldn't remember where he had been. He had me worried, if I'm honest, but there didn't seem to be anything wrong with him physically as far as I could tell. No bumps to the head or anything. After he pulled round, he insisted we get back to work. I kept asking if he was okay, but he said that he was. Thought he would have mentioned it to you. Nothing else happened really. Pete said he didn't much like where we were working. I didn't either. Can't really place why. But yeah, I have no idea where he went for those few hours because we searched everywhere.

Is he okay?

Travis.

~

I feel numb. Pete told me about a memory lapse, and that was worrying enough, but he didn't mention that he had disappeared during that time. And that seems like pretty important information that he should have shared.

Perhaps he plans to divulge that information later, but I still feel a pang of anger at the dishonesty. I even feel a little less guilty for sending the email in the first place. But, above all of that, there is just more worry. Where the hell did he disappear to during that time? And how could the people working there, especially Travis, lose him?

I don't get the chance to think things through further, or

formulate a reply, as I hear Pete make his way back downstairs.

6-9

I wake in the middle of the night again.

When I open my eyes, the first thing I do is quickly check Alfie's monitor to see that the baby is fine. But Alfie is not the reason I was pulled me from my sleep.

It's Pete.

Though he is still asleep, he is restless and talking.

'No. No. No. No. I won't.'

Even in the dark of night, I can see the sheen of sweat on his brow and the twisting of his face. His head flops one way, then the other, rolling from side to side on his pillow.

'No. No. No.'

I have no idea what he is dreaming about but, in that sub-conscious place, he is clearly struggling with something. I move a hand and rest it on his clammy shoulder in an effort to calm him. It doesn't work. His head still turns from one side to the other. I know I should wake him, but an idea enters my mind.

For whatever reason, Pete chose to withhold some details of his memory loss from me. Maybe if he can see how much he is slipping at the minute—because I have never seen him this fitful in his sleep—then perhaps I can break down the last of his resistance to being totally open with me. So I retrieve my phone and record him. The lack of light leaves the image very dark, so I switch my nightlight on to its lowest setting, making things more visible in my phone's viewfinder.

Pete continues to toss and turn. He pauses for a moment, breath seemingly caught. Then he shakes his head. 'No. No. No. I won't. I won't. No.'

I continue the recording for a few moments more before deciding I have enough. I don't want to embarrass Pete with this, just show how deeply things are affecting him at the minute, whether he realises it or not. I set the phone down and gently shake him.

'Pete,' I whisper as soothingly as I can. 'Pete, hun, wake up.' Another gentle shake, but it does nothing. What looked to be a fragile sleep is clearly deeper than I first thought. So I am more firm and vigorous in my attempts. 'Pete, wake up.'

Eventually, he stirs. His eyes open, and I see his pupils roll down from behind the lids.

'No. No.'

His voice is croaky and confused, and I can tell he is in that brief but maddening state between dream and reality, where the two blend and become one.

'It's okay,' I tell him. 'Be calm.'

He turns to me, and at first I am a stranger to him. His frown is evidence of that. But then, as his sleepy mind wakes more, I see the realisation draw over him.

'Cass?'

'Yeah, you were talking in your sleep.'

The words take a while to sink in. Then he rubs his eyes before pushing himself up to his elbows.

'I was?'

I nod. 'Yeah. You seemed distressed.'

'Weird,' he says with a shake of his head, the grogginess still clear in his voice.

'What were you dreaming about?'

He takes a moment. 'Can't really remember. I think I was in that church. But not an area I knew. A place underground that had opened itself up to me and...' He shakes his head. 'I don't know. It was stupid.'

'And who were you talking to?'

'What do you mean?'

'You were talking to someone. I heard you. So I wondered who it was.'

A shrug. 'No idea,' he says, but Pete has never been a very good liar. That statement, I know, wasn't quite true. It is written all over his face, confirmed by the way his eyes flick away from me, which is a clear tell. But I decide against it.

Not yet.

I debate whether to raise the issue of him going missing while away, as it seems a good time, considering what he has mentioned about his dream.

But Pete will not make eye contact and looks away from me, off to the dark corner of the room. I decide to not confront him about the important information he withheld from me, either. He looks sad and distant. Then, he frowns. His face drops, and his eyes glaze over.

'Pete?'

I nudge him, but he doesn't seem to notice. I follow his stare to the same corner. Though the darkness and shadows are deep enough so that I can't actually see where the walls meet, there doesn't seem to be anything of note over there.

'No,' he whispers, just as he did when dreaming. 'No.' I notice he is shaking slightly.

'Pete!' I say, raising my voice and shoving him a little

more forcefully. He seems to snap back into focus. He shakes his head, then looks over to me. 'What happened?' I ask.

Pete pauses for a moment. 'I don't know. I think I kind of zoned out.'

'Why were you saying the word 'no' over and over?'

'I was?' He looks genuinely surprised at this.

'Yes. You were.'

'I... I have no idea. I must be tired, I guess.' He lets his head flop back to the pillow behind. 'I just feel so... tired.'

Mere moments after he finishes that sentence, and before I have chance to reply, his eyes drift shut. I hear his breathing deepen, quickly turning into a light snore, and I realise that he's fallen asleep in the middle of taking to me. How that is even possible, I don't know.

Waking him probably isn't a good idea. If he fell asleep like that, then he isn't merely tired, but exhausted, so I don't want to break his sleep. But I feel deflated and angry, like things are building again and the dark waters are deepening all around us in our little boat of safety. And, no matter how much I try to scoop up that black liquid and cast it overboard, it feels like the bucket I am using has a hole in it, one that continues to grow the more I work.

I lie back down myself and let my eyes move over again to that same corner Pete was looking at.

I freeze. Something seems to move in the shadow. Something tall. A quick shifting of black on black.

No. Just in my head. Of course it was just in my head. Tired eyes and a tired mind. Christ, this is getting bad.

I try to stop what is building inside, but I don't succeed. Quiet sobs escape me.

6-10

I am surrounded by noises of normality: the steady hum of the shower running as Pete cleans himself in the bathroom, the chattering from Alfie through the monitor on my nightstand. And, if I listen carefully, I can actually distinguish between his noises through the device, and those that come directly from him, in through the open door of the master bedroom. He seems happy enough and would no doubt make it known when he had grown bored of his own company.

But I am tired.

My eyes feel dry, like a scattering of sand lines the fleshy orbs and scrapes against the insides of my eyelids with every blink. My head hurts. A throbbing, dull pain that emanates from the base of my skull.

The thought of leaving the comfort and safety of the bed seems like a Herculean task right now, so I decide to leave Alfie chattering in his room for a little bit longer. I just want to lie here and have a few precious moments to myself, where I can be sad and feel vulnerable. But soon I know that I will need to be strong again. For all of us.

Sleep is not an option, as there is not enough time before I will need to go get Alfie, so I instinctively reach for my phone and busy myself on social media, hoping it will act as a distraction from the problems that are eating away at the back of my mind. Problems I know I can't ignore for long.

But social media does not work as a time-suck for me, and I am unable to hold my focus. Instead, I go to my videos, remembering the recording I took of Pete last night, of him talking in his sleep. I listen carefully before hitting 'play,' and can still hear the water running from the shower, so I start the recording, with the sound turned up slightly in order to hear, confident I have time to see the full playback before Pete finishes up.

As expected, the footage is dark, but I can still make out Pete, his head flopping one way then the other. Then the nightlight comes on and the video becomes a little clearer, but not by much. I know that soon, Pete will speak in his sleep. But, before that happens, I hear something else, something that makes me pause in confusion. And something, I realise, that I did not hear at the time of recording.

'*Per me.*'

The voice is deep and guttural, distorted, and almost... otherworldly. And it sounds very, very ominous.

And then I hear Pete's voice, dazed and hypnotic, 'No. No. No. I won't. I won't. No.' Last night, I assumed he was just muttering while in a dream state. And while that may be the case, the timing of Pete talking seems like too much of a coincidence. I can only think that it was a direct response to this unknown speaker.

Per me.

The same words I heard through the baby monitor the night before last. At the time I'd dismissed it. But, after playing the recording back, and hearing that horrible voice speak again, there can be no mistake. After the first exchange, I hear the phrase repeat.

'*Per me.*'

Then, again, Pete's reply, 'No. No. No.'

A creeping feeling runs up my spine. The video finishes, a frozen image of Pete's troubled, sleeping face. And then, I see it. The creeping feeling intensifies, blooming out into absolute fear that runs to my very finger tips and toes. I want to gasp, but find it difficult to take a breath.

Though it is blurry in the paused image—quality worsened and distorted by the low light—there is no mistaking it.

Something could be seen. It was tall, lurking in the deep shadows of the corner of the room directly behind Pete.

6-11

'I know how it sounds,' I tell my mother, who is on the other end of the landline, 'but I'm scared.'

I sit looking at the screen of my mobile phone. It displays the paused image of the previous night's video and that... thing... is visible.

'But you have to realise how it sounds,' my mother says from the other end of the phone line. Her tone is as soft and understanding as she can make it, but I can sense her annoyance. In terms of believing in the more fantastical things in life, I've always taken more after my late father than her. Mother, bless her soul, is much more of a sceptic and more a realist. Well, scepticism is putting it lightly. She thought it was all bullshit.

I set the mobile phone down onto the breakfast bar and swap the landline receiver to my other ear, stretching my neck out as I do, fighting against a cramp that was building. In the days of mobile phones, landlines became something of a novelty, but Mother always makes a point of calling on it, preferring the stability that was sometimes missing from the cellular devices, which could drop their signal without notice. She also doesn't care for the way cell phones are—in her words—making us all mindless zombies, all staring at these little devices and their small screens instead of looking up at the world around us.

'I know,' I finally say after a moment's pause. And that is true, I do know how ridiculous it all sounds. But I am also still looking at the frozen picture of that unexplainable thing, and—ridiculous or not—I have to believe my own eyes.

'I think you need to put that rubbish out of your head,' my mother says. 'There are likely a million and one sane ways to explain it. Concentrate on Pete. If you say he looks like he's having a slip, then concentrate on trying to help and fix that.'

'I can't just fix it, Mum,' I tell her.

'I know it must be hard, dear, but you have to try.'

'No, that isn't what I mean. It's not that I don't want to. I mean it doesn't work that way. His depression isn't something you can fix just like that.'

'Okay,' she replies, softy and patiently. 'Then just be there for him. Talk things through. You've got a lot on your plate, hun. I can't imagine how stressful everything must be for you both. But you'll get through it. You are strong. So is Pete. You make him strong. Just recognise that you are in a dip right now, but you won't stay there.'

Her words make sense to me. Well, mostly they do. But at the same time, I can't just ignore what I am looking at, what is clear on the screen of my phone.

I decide I need to speak with Pete, to gain some measure of what he knows about this, if anything.

He had taken Alfie to the park a little over an hour ago, asking if I wanted to go as well. Part of me did, as staying in the house didn't seem appealing—I felt on edge, my mind always running back to that damned recording. But I told him no, I was tired, and I could do with a little 'me time.' I could tell by the look on his face he sensed something was up, but was kind enough to leave it and take Alfie out by himself. Truth is, I needed time away from him, to speak with someone else.

And, though being here alone gave me the feeling I was being watched, nothing actually happened. So I called the only other person in the world I could confide in with absolutely anything. Though, given her factual and evidence-based view of the world, I should have expected a less than understanding response when telling her what I'd heard and seen.

I may have been better off phoning Pete's older sister on that front, who is much more of a 'believing' person when it comes to the unexplained. Indeed, I remember her once telling me of Pete's birth, how he had a fleshy caul over his face after being born. A sign, their mother had insisted, that he was blessed with 'the sight.' A kind of psychic ability. Pete flatly refuted this when his sister raised it again recently, even getting angry at the insinuation.

'If I had that kind of ability, don't you think I'd have stopped what happened to them?'

That was an awkward dinner.

And it was also the first time I learned of how Pete's parents had died—house fire, when he was younger. He and his sister made it out, though he was badly burned in the process, and their parents were not so lucky.

'Hun?' Mother asks, pulling me from my wandering thoughts.

'Yeah?'

'You there? You went quiet on me.'

'Sorry, just thinking things through.' I hear the front

door open, signalling Pete and Alfie's return. 'Listen, I have to go. But I'll talk to you soon. And thanks.'

I end the call and walk through to the entrance hallway to see Pete wheeling the pram to a stop and closing the front door behind him. He brings a finger up to his lips and points to the pram, indicating Alfie is asleep. I smile and nod. We leave Alfie to nap and retreat into the kitchen.

'Drink?' I ask.

'I could go for a coffee,' he tells me.

I prepare myself one as well. 'Enjoy the park?' I ask.

'Yeah. It was great. You should have come.'

'I know,' I say. 'Just wasn't really feeling up to it. I didn't sleep too well, so just wanted to stay here and take it easy.'

Pete nods. He looks like he is going to say something, but then stops. I bring his coffee to him as he sits at the breakfast bar, then I set it down and take a sip of my own. It is piping hot and full-flavoured. I savour it. My phone still lies on the countertop, sitting between us, and I can't help myself. I have been wavering on whether to show him, thinking it best not raise the whole thing, but I dearly need answers.

'What happened while you were away?' I ask.

After taking a long drink of his own, Pete looks up, confused. 'What do you mean?'

'When you went missing. What happened?'

Pete's face drops in surprise. Even, I notice, a tinge of anger. 'How did you know about that?' he eventually asks.

My first thought is to lie, because how I know isn't important. That it happened, and what has happened since, is what we need to talk about. But I've been a little deceitful myself and gone behind his back, and I do not want that to continue. I've already started this conversation now, so it is too late to turn back.

'I emailed Travis,' I tell him. 'I've been worried about you, ever since you've come back.'

'I'm fine,' he says, raising his voice.

'You aren't!' I shoot back.

'Yes I am!' he shouts. 'Look, I'm sorry about what happened the other night. I really am. But I apologised for it then, and I've booked in to see Dr. Caryll. I don't see why you had to go snooping around and checking up on me.'

'And I don't see why you didn't just tell me that you went missing and couldn't even remember what happened. I mean Jesus, Pete, that's a pretty big thing. You should have been honest with me. I can't help you if you shut me out.'

He shakes his head. I can see his jaw tense as his teeth clench together. 'You can't help me by going behind my back!'

I stop, even though I want to continue. This isn't all down to me, and I don't want to be made a scapegoat, when all I am trying to do is to help. But to bite back, to allow an argument to unfold, will only make things worse. Besides, I still want to show him that video recording, and what is on it. I want to talk about what I heard on the baby monitor the other night. And I want to discuss the fact that—as crazy as it sounds—there is something else going on here. Something not easily believable. But I don't get the chance.

'I need to go out again,' he states.

'What do you mean?'

'I just need to clear my head. I'm going for a walk.'

'But—'

'I won't be long,' he tells me, then leaves, leaving me alone with the baby.

I cry, feeling like everything is unravelling. All our hard work though those difficult times, and all the good we now have in our life, is starting to untangle and fall away.

Alfie starts to cry.

Pete returns a few hours later, as he said, but we don't speak much. His frosty silence makes it clear that it is not something he is willing to resolve just yet. He shouldn't have been able to make that decision on his own, but I am too exhausted to push things any further today.

Tomorrow will be another day and another chance at putting things right.

Pete falls to sleep easily that night. And, even with everything going on in my head, sleep finds me quickly as well. But the next thing I know, I am once again pulled from my slumber.

It's the dead of night. All is quiet except the quiet sound of sobbing. It's Pete, but he isn't beside me anymore.

I shriek in horror as I see him above me, inexplicably pinned to the ceiling, his eyes wide with terror.

Pete's arms are by his side and his body, floating above me, looks to be locked rigid.

The pure horror and panic etched into his expression—his eyes pleading for help—is terrifying to me, and I can't make sense of what I am seeing. Pete is pressed up against the ceiling, unable to move other than to shake in fear.

This is impossible. Impossible. This can't be real.

I feel as immobilised as he clearly is, frozen by the sheer terror that has seized my limbs.

'Pete...' I say, but my voice is little more than a shaky whisper.

'Help,' he whispers back. I see tears drip down from his cheeks. This spurs me into action. Finding a courage I didn't know I had in the face of this insanity, I climb to my feet on the bed, reaching up to my husband. I take hold of him by the shoulders—his skin feels ice cold, so much so that it stings my fingertips—and start to heave at him. There is no movement. Not even an inch. I scream—both with fear and exertion—as I desperately try to pull against whatever force is holding him like this. Still he cries. Still his wet eyes are wide in absolute terror.

And then they roll back in his head, showing only the whites beneath. A long exhale escapes his lips, and his body seems to relax. Then, Pete drops.

I try to embrace him as he falls, but the weight is too much, and we both crash down to the bed, him landing on top of me. All I can think of as his weight momentarily pins me down is that exhale he emitted—long and raspy—and the way his eyes sunk back.

Is he dead?

I quickly wriggle my way out from under him, rolling him to his back, and check his breathing. I heave a sigh of relief. I can see his chest rise and fall and feel the warmth of the breath coming from his nose. His skin, too, starts to regain more of its natural warmth, replacing the biting cold that consumed it only moments ago.

'Wake up,' I plead with him, shaking him violently. Fear still grips me. I know that we need to flee this place. There is no natural explanation for what just happened. We are in danger. Him, me, and Alfie.

We must go.

But I feel that, in order to make the short distance downstairs and out of the house, I need Pete by my side to protect me. Protect us. I can't do it alone.

But Pete does not move. He is completely unconscious, and I am unable to rouse him. I consider it is possible that he could be in a coma.

I then hear Alfie start to cry through the monitor. To scream, in fact. I look up to the display and see him kicking in his crib. Then I see a shadow fall over his form.

Another voice comes through, overpowering the screams of my son.

'*Per me.*'

6-13

The insanity of everything is almost too much to bear, and my mind struggles to keep up. My heart is pounding in my chest, and I know I need to get to my child out of this house. I get to my feet—legs like jelly, like they may give out under me at any moment—and run to Alfie's room. As I sprint I brace myself, fully expecting to see... something... in his room. But I find nothing. Only Alfie. Still screaming.

I scoop him up and hold him close.

'It's okay,' I whisper, not really believing it. Then I hear that voice again. It booms out. But not from this room. From the master bedroom. A horrible, demonic sound, surely not of this world.

'*Per me.*'

I need to get out of here. The thought of leaving Pete behind tears at my heart, but what choice do I have? I don't even care about my own safety. Right now I only care about Alfie, and about getting him out of here. I don't really understand what the hell is happening, but I can sense a building and terrifying danger.

So I run out of the room... and stop.

Pete is standing in the hallway, facing me, stock still and completely naked. His eyes are closed, and I can see the glistening of sweat on his body.

'Pete?'

He doesn't respond. Just stands motionless, like a statue, blocking my route to the stairs.

I take a tentative step forward. 'Let me through,' I say, quietly but firmly.

He doesn't respond. Then, beyond him, I hear something. A whisper, cracked and hoarse. '*Per me. Per me. Per me.*'

'No,' he replies, his voice little more than a whisper itself.

Then, a horrible sound rings out all around us. A booming and deep roar filled with hate and anger. Pete's eyes snap open. For a moment, he looks confused.

'Cass? What... what's happening?'

I don't have time to answer as the unknown force again hoists Pete up into the air. He hangs vertically, facing me, and a look of terror crosses his face. Then his arms are quickly pulled up to his side, splaying out, and his legs are forced apart as well, leaving him spread-eagle in mid-air.

'Help me!' he screams.

But I have no idea how.

6-14

'Pete!' I yell and take a tentative step towards him. I hold out a hand and touch his skin. Again, it is ice-cold.

'Cassie...' he says. 'I can't stop it.'

'Stop what?'

'It wants us. It wants Alfie. And it needs to come through me to get him.'

'*Per me.*'

There it was again—loud and angry. The wall-mounted pictures in the hallway shake on their hooks as the reverberations of the terrible words carry on long after they should have dissipated. Then, the unseen entity speaks again, this time in English.

'*Let. Me. Through.*'

'No!' Pete cries out. 'I won't! You hear me? Never! So leave us alone! Just—'

Pete stops and his jaw falls open, eyes suddenly open wide. The scream of pain that erupts from his mouth will stay with me forever. It takes me a moment to realise what is happening, but then I see it, the bulge of movement just beneath his skin, at the base of his rib-cage to the left-hand side.

The bottom bone of the rib-cage begins to twist upwards, lapping over the one above it. Pete continues to cry and writhe and scream in absolute agony as he is held aloft, unable to pull down his arms stop what is happening to him. Alfie continues to cry in my arms, and I feel like my mind is about to shatter.

I hear a sudden snap as the twisting end of the bone breaks from the strain, and I see it pivot completely, pointing almost directly upwards. The end of the bone punctures through the skin, revealing a sharp end smeared with blood. Pete's screams continue, and I notice the bone to the base of the right-hand side begins to turn as well, mimicking what has just happened to the left.

Whatever has Pete in this unseeable grasp is inflicting a slow and deliberate torture on him.

'*Per me.*'

'No,' Pete wheezes out. 'No!'

Then I see it. The thing that has been tormenting my husband—and by extension, the rest of us—since he returned. And it is more hideous and terrifying than I could have ever imagined.

Ghost, demon, or monster, I have no idea. The only thing I am certain of is that this... thing... is not human. Not natural. It is something else entirely.

It steps out from the third bedroom at the end of the hallway, behind Pete, and ducks under the door frame before pulling itself up to a standing position, though it has to stoop its vile head below the ceiling given its unnatural height. Its spindly, drooping body is a mixture of charred black and sore red flesh. The skin is bubbled with puss-filled pockets, weeping with a thick substance. The demon looks like it has stepped out of an inferno. Indeed, a horrible smell permeates the area—that of cooking meat.

That red and black skin stretches over a protruding, almost exaggerated pot belly that hangs low, almost covering its exposed small and flaccid penis.

On the head of this nightmare are wisps of straggly and greasy grey hair. Much of its face is hidden by a flap of membrane—like skin, with deep purple veins beneath. A single eye and half of the mouth are all that is visible beneath this caul, but I can easily make out a wild and lustful expression. It giggles in wild excitement and begins to stroke its limp penis.

It then takes a step forward, gyrating its hips as it moves, thrusting its member into its palm, again and again. But the organ gives no response, flapping uselessly inside of the thing's grasp. The demon continues walking and playing with itself until it reaches my Pete, standing directly behind him.

'*Let. Me. Through.*'

Pete shakes his head as he continues to moan in agony. 'Never.'

'Pete!' I cry. 'What should I do?' I had no idea how to help my husband—the love of my life—in the face of such horror. I feel trapped and helpless and terrified.

'Nothing,' he wheezes out. 'If I don't let it, then it can't do anything to you.'

'But it's killing you.'

Pete screams again as the monster takes hold of his head and squeezes.

'*Let. Me. Through.*'

'No!' Pete screams defiantly. The thing gives out an inhuman roar but eventually releases the pressure on his head.

It is too much for me. The fear and panic overwhelm me, and I feel my legs give out as I drop to the floor. Thankfully, I am able to keep Alfie secure as I land on my rear, and I cradle him close as I then kick myself backwards and press my back into the wall behind me.

'Let him go!' I scream.

'Cass...' Pete whispers. 'Don't look.'

'What do you mean?'

'Look away... It knows I won't give in.' His words are strained.

'Good. Fight the fucker,' I say. 'Don't give in. Tell it to go back to hell.'

'It won't go quietly... Close your eyes, baby.'

'No!' I cry. 'Don't give up!'

'I'm not giving up,' he says with a sad smile. 'I know what's going to happen. But I'll hold the darkness back. I'm stronger than it is.'

I start to cry harder as the realisation of what he is saying to me hits home. How can I ready myself for what is going to happen?

'Close... your eyes,' he says.

The demon leans its head in closer to Pete, its large hands pressing again on his head. '*Let. Me. Through.*'

Pete grits his teeth together. 'Go... to... hell!'

I close my eyes. Over Alfie's screaming, I hear Pete's awful cries of agony build and build and build... until they are suddenly silenced by a sickening and wet crunch.

I then hear his body hit the floor. All is quiet.

I open my eyes, and they run with even more tears as I see what is left of my husband, lying prone on the floor, his head now no more than a gory red mush pooled at the end of his neck.

The demon is gone.

I scream until my voice gives out.

I take a sip of the warm tea that my mother brought me. Today has been a better day. Yesterday was a bad one. All I could think of was Pete and what we went through in his final hours. How he was pulled away from me by something impossible. That was four months ago now.

The unfairness of the whole fucking thing is not something I will ever come to terms with.

But today Alfie has been very active and playful, and interacting with him has helped to block out the memory that otherwise haunts me.

Explaining what happened to the police was an ordeal. Of course it was, how could it not be? How do you tell law enforcement that your husband had his head crushed by a demon that seemed to have followed him back from some ancient church he was working in? A demon that wanted to use him to get to me and my baby.

The simple fact was, I couldn't explain it. Not without being put away and having my baby taken from me.

So I didn't tell them that. I lied. Told them I heard someone break in. Pete put me and the baby in our room and went out to confront whoever it was. I told them I didn't know what happened exactly, but heard a horrific struggle. Everything died down, and I said that at that point I was sure the other person—or people, I couldn't be sure—had fled, and that I came out to see my husband in the state the police found him in after I called them.

They couldn't explain what would have caused such injuries, and I don't know how much they believed my story, but I was free, and Alfie was with me. The last update I received from the police was that they had not managed to find any suspects and, given the lack of evidence, that might not change. I pretended to be angry at that, and said I wanted justice for my husband's murder. But I know that is impossible.

Pete gave his life for Alfie and me. Resisted unimaginable pain and torture and mental anguish; looked that blackness directly in the eye when it demanded to be let through, and defiantly told it 'no.' I was immensely proud of that, but that pride didn't replace the hole in my heart that was left after he died.

I want him here with me. With Alfie. And here for the child that now grows in my womb.

Alfie giggles up at me with a smile that is all Pete. I smile back.

THE BLACK FOREST

7-1

Scotland - 1627
Eileen

I'm tired. So very tired.

My joints ache, and the walking is hard. But it is something we must do. Our last settlement proved to be less than adequate—the land too poor for our needs and our crops to grow. So, with heavy hearts, we packed up and moved on, ready to begin again.

But, before we settle, we must find a suitable place to claim for our own and once again try and lay down some roots. Which is why we now march through these dense woods. Our town elder, Henry, believes there may be a settlement on the other side. One that we could, hopefully, join. But these woods in which we find ourselves unnerve me. They seem to go on forever, and I cannot shake the feeling that we are being watched as we move, as if some unknown *thing* studies us from the darkness between the trees.

Because of that, amongst other things, I can't help but

think that the hike through this forest is a mistake. I spoke to Henry about it, but the once wise man now only takes council from his new wife.

Agnes Sibbett.

A woman new to our group. We found her alone, and Henry took pity on her, though I could tell it was more than that. It wasn't just pity. It was lust. I've seen the look in men before that he gave to Agnes when he decreed she would join our community. I've not experienced that look aimed at myself, I should say, but I have indeed seen it, regardless.

Henry was himself married at the time when Agnes joined us, but Joan—a lady I respected greatly—succumbed to a strange injury that subsequently ended her life. She'd been hurt in an accident no one was able to explain. Henry used it as another reason to say the land we were originally settled in was impure. It had not taken him long to take Agnes Sibbett as his new wife, the two of them making the declaration to us all, with an abundance of witnesses to confirm the union.

But Agnes Sibbett's sudden rise in our small hierarchy is not the only reason I distrust that woman. There is something not right about her. When she talks, she stares so intently as to peer into one's soul. She doesn't blink much and—as I like to think I am a sound judge of character—I can detect no warmth or humanity in her.

She never fully explained to us where she came from, which settlement she belonged to before wandering into ours, or what indeed happened to that group. If she had told Henry the details of these mysteries, he had not relayed such knowledge to me or anyone I am friendly with.

Even poor George is wary of her, and he is one of the kindest people in our cluster of souls. He is one of the young lads in our group, a child really, even though he says he is a man. However, he does not have the required years behind him, or the masculine build, to make such claims. But he has a disposition that is both sunny and positive, and I have never seen anyone so much as raise their voice to him in anger, never mind hold some kind of grudge. Yet Agnes Sibbett had the boy in tears only recently, after—according to him—senselessly killing his small dog. Sibbett denied it, and Henry believed her, and that was the end of the matter. But George swore on his life that he was telling the truth, and I have no reason to doubt or distrust the boy.

Unlike that foul woman, Agnes Sibbett.

In an effort to raise his spirits, I have let George take charge of my kid goat, Ollie, in the hope it will take his mind from the loss of his own pet. It seems to have worked so far, at least a little. Ollie, of course, will have value to the village —wherever we decide settle—beyond being a mere pet. All of the animals we have with us—the few that have not been wiped out by disease—have a purpose. But for now, I do look at little Ollie as a small, happy companion. One I am willing to share with poor George.

And so we move on, through the mass of trees that never seem to end. The tiredness grows. Though Henry claims otherwise, I know we will have to spend yet another night here in these cursed woods. And perhaps more beyond that.

The mood in our group is low. Trust in Henry, I feel, is wavering. But for now, we march on.

The night is cold. We have kept a large fire going, and most sleep round it, but there are too many of us to all fit around it. Some can't find room close enough to feel any warmth from the flames, myself included, and I spent a few hours cold and aching, feeling the chill worm its way into my bones. Sleep was elusive and, before long, the need to relieve myself was too great, so I stood and moved away from the warm light of the fire and out into the trees to find privacy. After answering the call of nature, I was about to make my way back to the huddle when movement up ahead in the dark caught my attention.

My first instinct is to run straight back to the others. After all, I have no idea what dangers lurk in these woods. However, I soon come to the realisation that it is a person, and they are whispering. I creep closer, keeping myself low, curiosity getting the better of me. Surely it has to be some of our own party out there, but I can only make out a single figure... So who are they whispering to?

Closer still and I realise that the person is female, dressed in dark colours, with scraggly, dark hair on her head. I recognise her now. It is Agnes, and she is facing out into the trees. The words she is whispering—that I can make out—are odd, and I am unable to hear full sentences. However, she seems to be supplicating to... something.

'Yes. Of course. My life is yours.'

Very strange.

And, in her hands, a small bird, with what looks to be a lame wing. I wonder if, for a moment, she had plucked it from the ground to help the poor creature. But she grabs it by the neck and twists suddenly, sneering as she does. I hear a small *crack,* and I let out a gasp.

She hears this and turns. 'Who's there?'

It is pointless trying to hide, and, in all honesty, I don't wish to. I am angered at what I have just seen—such pointless aggression at something so helpless. I didn't doubt George's story before, but now there is no room for doubt in my mind about what happened to his poor dog.

'It is me,' I say. I don't give my name and am not sure if she even knows it. Her smile grows deeper.

Darker.

She begins to walk over and discards the body of the small bird to the ground.

'Ah, the mewling little worm of our fair family. Eileen, is it?'

Faced with this confident and confrontational attitude—which I have to admit, takes me off guard—I can feel myself shrink back, and I hate being so timid. The brief jolt of bravery and anger I felt at her previous actions lilts away when I need them to grow stronger.

'Yes,' I say, trying my best to sound strong. Agnes walks right up to me, her mouth still pulled wide in a humourless grin. I truly cannot fathom what Henry, our leader, sees in this woman. She is not beautiful, in my honest opinion, because she does not possess the required warmth for that. And, on a surface level, too, her frame and face are gaunt, her nose long and hooked. Though, perhaps, that is my jealously talking, given I have had no male attention to speak of in my entire life.

'The wilting and untouched runt of the group,' Agnes sneers, taunting me further. 'Tell me, are you lost?'

I shake my head. 'No. Who were you talking to?'

'No one.'

'And why did you kill that bird?'

'Because I wanted to,' Agnes replies, as if it is the most obvious thing in the world. 'And there is no one to stop me.'

There is something seriously wrong with this woman. 'Is that why you killed George's dog, too?'

Agnes Sibbett just laughs, then moves past me. 'I am going to get some rest now. But a word of warning, little worm: do not snoop after me. If you intrude in my business again, well, accidents do happen.'

And then she walks away, back to the group, leaving me stunned and scared at the rather unambiguous threat levelled at me. I stand alone for a few moments, trying to gather myself and determined not to cry.

Two days have passed since my confrontation with Agnes Sibbett. We wander still through this damn forest, aimless, with no end in sight. It makes no sense. Surely it is not so big that we wouldn't have broken through by now. And yet, here we are, still marching through and following the lead of our esteemed leader. Or, rather, his new wife. Who, it seems, has taken charge of directing us on this merry trek.

After a morning of hiking, we break for food and rest. The 'banquet' consists of green beans and nuts. The last of the corn from our previous settlement is now all but gone, and no one is getting enough food, really. There is many a gaunt and disheveled face as people greedily consume what little they have.

No one seems happy. Yet, at the same time, no one speaks up to give voice to their discontent.

As I eat, Maria—a perfectly pleasant young woman with whom I talk frequently—shuffles next to me to confide something. I notice that she looks as pale as I have ever seen anyone, and I wonder briefly if she is ill.

'Something is wrong with that woman,' Maria whispers,

eyes wide. I don't have to ask who she is talking about. But I do anyway.

'Who do you mean?'

'Her,' Maria whispers, pointing over to Henry, and to his new wife, who sits next to him, grinning without showing emotion. 'Sibbett.'

I nod. 'I do agree. Something about her does not sit well with me.'

'Not just that. I think she is in league with evil.'

I turn to face her, certain my face shows the surprise I am feeling. 'What? How do you mean?'

'I mean... there is something in this forest. Something unnatural. I felt it when we first entered. Didn't you?' I don't answer, though part of me agrees with what the girl is saying. She goes on, 'And last night... I saw something.'

'What?' I ask in a conspiratorial whisper, feeling myself lean in to the girl who was, herself, speaking in hushed tones.

The girl points at Sibbett again. 'Her. She was out in the trees, alone. I saw her sneak off. So I followed her. She was talking to the very air itself. Muttering things that made no sense. Madness.' That sounds familiar, and my thoughts run back to my own encounter with Agnes Sibbett in the middle of the night. 'But it gets worse,' Maria continues. 'I don't know if I can make sense of what I saw next.'

The girl's quiet voice is unsteady, and I can hear the fear in her words. She went on, 'I followed her deeper into the woods, listening to her whisper to no one. And then she came to a tree—a big one with a thick base, biggest one I've seen here. She walked around the trunk to the other side, and waited. And... I swear I'm telling you the truth... I saw something come out of that tree. Can't describe what it was. Like insanity given form. Not human. *Beyond* human. And it reached out to Agnes. Not with arms, but with something else. Slithering things. And it pulled her into it, into the tree, I think. My legs gave out and I fell. I crawled away, scared for my life, and, when I had strength enough in my legs again, I ran. Came back to the group. But Sibbett showed up later. I saw her sneak back in amongst us, like nothing had happened. But I know what happened, Eileen, I *know* what I saw. Something is out there in this forest, something old and evil, and I just know that it took Agnes Sibbett. For a little while, at least.'

I sat in silence, unsure what to think. Maria is not the type of person to lie or spread needless or nasty stories about people. But the tale she has just told me—if true—is terrifying. What was I supposed to think?

'We need to watch her,' Maria adds. 'And we need to get out of this forest, quickly. If we stay here, we will die. Or go mad. But no good will come from being here any longer.'

Regardless of what I thought of Maria's story, I cannot disagree with that last notion. We *need* to be away from this dreadful place.

However, I have a horrible feeling that the woman who entered our lives recently and worked her way to the head of our community would make that quite difficult.

'Settling here?' I ask, incredulous. 'In these woods? That cannot be true.'

'It's what I heard,' George replies. 'Andrew told me that his mother overheard Agnes Sibbett talking about it with Henry, telling him it was the only thing that made sense. Said it would be the perfect place for us, protected by the trees.'

'But we can't settle in a forest. We need fields for crops and room for cattle.'

George just shrugs and repeats himself. 'It's what I heard.'

Of course, I don't disbelieve George—he has no reason to lie to me—but the thought of staying in this forest *permanently* was just beyond reason. And to hear that Henry has agreed to this madness is just too much to listen to. He has to be made to see sense. I decide to speak to Henry directly, and alone.

It takes until later that evening, as the night has begun to set in, but I eventually manage to find him keeping his own company. I approach him.

'Henry, may I speak with you?'

He studies me. 'Aye,' he replies with a nod, looking slightly annoyed at being interrupted. Henry is a tall man and towers over me. He is well set with raging red hair and a wild beard.

'I've heard whisperings that it is our intention to settle our new village here, in these woods.'

Henry chuckles. 'People around here talk a lot.'

'Is it true?'

His gaze bores into me, making me shrink back. It is a stern stare, one that struggles to mask a bubbling anger. 'Aye, it's true,' he eventually says.

Even though I half expected him to answer in the affirmative, I still can't quite believe it. 'Henry,' I say, 'that is madness. We can't settle in a forest. We don't have the room. How will we build here? How will we grow crops or raise cattle? We can't—'

'Enough!' he shouts, cutting me off. 'I will not be questioned by the likes of you. Do you understand?' I simply stand with my mouth open, in complete shock. 'I said,' he goes on, gritting his teeth and taking a step towards me, 'do you understand?' I nod. 'Good,' he adds. 'Now, to answer your questions, we will make the room we require by felling trees as we need to. And we will use the timber from those trees to build. We will use what the forest provides us and create a life here.'

'But why? Why not leave this place behind, as was the original intent?'

'Agnes has made me see the benefits of living here. And she is right. So, I will tell you this only once: *this* is where we settle. If you don't like it, then move on alone. I will make an announcement to everyone else tonight, and they will fall in line. If you want to cause trouble, however, then you will be dealt with accordingly. So do what you are good at, Eileen—keep your head down and mouth shut.'

And with that, he brushes past me and walks away. For the second time in days I have to fight not to burst into tears. What is happening to our leader, and our community? Surely the others will see the madness in this course of action and turn away?

As it was, just as Henry suggested, everyone fell in line, afraid to speak up against him and his inner circle. We chose a location within the forest—at the base of a steep incline—and over the course of the following months, we began to fell trees and build our village here in this forest of the damned.

Two years later...

'It was a mistake agreeing to it all,' Robert says from his seated position on the log next to me. Maria flanks me on the opposite side. These little conspiratorial conversations have become commonplace between a certain few of us. 'The whole thing is a cursed mistake. And now we are trapped.'

He is right, of course, but the problem is, we *did* agree to it. All of us. Despite our doubts and worries, the collective community gave in to the easier option of letting another person decide our future. It is always easier letting others make difficult decisions, and actually takes a surprising amount of bravery to turn away from that. Bravery—it seemed—that none of us had.

And now there are some of us that regret it. Robert more than most, as his dear sweet wife—Anna—died only three months prior, succumbing to a disease that has thinned out our numbers. And yet, we all still follow like sheep as Henry, guided by Agnes, becomes more strong-willed than ever.

Though it has taken many months, as a group we have

actually managed to build homes in the forest, using the felled trees for the timber houses—just as Henry envisioned. In truth, the idea of a town in amongst the trees has been more workable than I first imagined, once the backbreaking task of clearing the area of trees was accomplished. There is also a stream close to us for water, but Henry insisted—at Agnes' behest—that we dig a well in the centre of the small village that we constructed. To everyone's surprise, we actually hit water, though the first of what was brought up was closer to black sludge. When that cleared, however, it seemed we had a reliable water source. The animals in the forest, too, became a good source of food, as did the foliage. And the predictions made by Henry and his ever more secretive wife all seem to come to pass with alarming frequency. This, of course, has led many of the village-folk to throw all of their trust in with Henry and the other elders. And, of course, with Agnes. Who—it has become clear—is becoming the true leader of us all.

So, considering that the start of our lives settled in the forest was actually better than feared—save the disease that took the lives of a fifth of our number—there is a significant portion of the township, myself included, that does not want to be here. Because, as Maria said to me two years ago: *There is something in this forest. Something unnatural.*

I truly believe that now.

At first, I tried to put some of the things I was feeling down to simply not knowing the environment.

The noises. The changes in temperature. The oppressive feel of the overbearing trees that tower above us. Things that are all different to the open fields I was used to. But I can no longer ignore what is becoming increasingly obvious.

The sound of whispering in the night from deep within

the forest cannot be put down to a natural occurrence. And sometimes, when I look out from my window and into the tree-line beyond our village, when night is at its deepest, I see figures out there in the dark. Horrible and nightmarish things; twisted, gruesome and unholy. At first, I thought I was succumbing to some sickness that was causing hallucinations. Then, others confided in me that they had seen the same.

And one recent incident shook me to my core. I was awakened in the night by the noise of someone moving outside of my small home. I peered over to the window in my bedroom and—to my horror—saw someone standing outside, looking back in, their face just outside of the glass.

Whatever was out there, it was a nightmarish sight, with the distorted and ruined features of a corpse long since dead. However, this living corpse was recognisable to me. Robert's deceased wife.

Anna.

After screaming myself hoarse, and refusing to talk to the neighbours who came to my aid, I have decided to keep that story to myself for fear it will spread panic. But now, looking at Robert and his haggard and tired expression, I do wonder if he has seen the same.

'We could leave,' I say. It is something I have thought about many times over the last two years, but it is not something I have ever acted on, as there is little chance of us surviving out there on our own. So I've never raised the notion of it with anyone. However, things are different now. They are getting worse. 'We could leave for Amaley or Brumeer.'

Amaley and Brumeer are towns that have recently become known to us, which exist outside of the forest, but which are, I think, reachable. Indeed, after initial tradings between our village and their towns, there was talk of deepening those connections in order to bring in the resources that we need.

And while some elders saw merit in this, and pushed for more trade, Agnes—and Henry by extension—were resistant.

'Possibly,' Maria says. 'But the trek would be a long and arduous one.'

'It would. But surely it would be worth it to get away from here? Those of us who wish to leave can do so, and others can stay behind to the life they want.'

'A comforting thought,' Robert says with a solemn nod. 'And tempting. But we must be cautious. You know what I think of this forest, and the things that lurk here. I believe we are of similar minds on that. But I do not think that whatever darkness resides here would let us leave so easily.' He then extends a hand and points into the centre of town, where Agnes Sibbett is giving directions to a group of men. 'Especially her. I have a feeling she, in particular, would rather see people die than abandon her leadership.'

'If we stay here then we will likely die anyway,' Maria says.

'What is she telling them, anyway?' I ask, gesturing to a section of land in the centre of the town, where Agnes is still delivering her instructions.

'Haven't you heard?' Robert asks. 'She means to build a church here. And Henry has agreed.'

I shake my head. 'Never took her as a woman of God.'

'She ain't,' Robert replies. 'I have a feeling that the church she wants isn't intended for the Lord.'

'We are going to do it,' Maria tells me. 'Tonight.'

I feel myself tense up, worried we will be overheard. A silly concern, given we are alone out in the forest, and away from the village—the two of us tasked with foraging for berries and other edibles. It has been only two days since the discussion between Robert, Maria, and me on the log in the village.

'But it's so quick,' I reply. 'Is everyone prepared?'

'As much as we can be,' Maria states. 'We can't risk anyone else discovering what we are planning, so Robert has said we need to leave. And it is to be tonight. So... are you coming?'

I don't know how to respond. I knew of the plan: a small number of the villagers planned to leave and head to one of the closest towns outside of the forest, and I had suggested that I'd be agreeable to leaving with them. It was my idea originally, anyway. But I didn't expect things to move so quickly. Originally, they talked about making sure they had what they needed for the journey before leaving in a week's time.

'I... I don't know.'

'What don't you know, Eileen?' Maria asks, visibly surprised at my response. 'Do you want to stay here then? Live under the rule of Sibbett? You will be lucky if you see next spring.'

I know Maria is right, of course, but if I am honest, I am scared. This is all just too sudden, and a flurry of questions bubbles up in my mind. What if we aren't ready? We don't really know how long this forest goes on for, and what if we don't have enough supplies? And, most troubling of all, what if Agnes Sibbett and her inner circle know what we are planning? Would she just let us leave?

I remain silent, so Maria goes on. 'We leave tonight, when all is still and people are asleep in their homes. We will gather outside of town, just beyond the crest of the hill. If you want to come, meet us there, but make sure you are quiet and do not draw attention. If not, stay here with whatever evil lives in this blasted forest. But we are going, with or without you.'

She seems angry, as if my reservations are somehow an affront to her, and she says no more. Instead, she simply heaves up her basket—half-full with the results of her foraging—and walks back towards the village on her own.

I have a decision to make—and both options scare me terribly. The thought of being left behind in this place, without the support of those I have grown to trust and confide in, makes me feel nauseous. Like I would be left with wolves who would soon turn on me. But, at the same time, the notion of trying to escape and being caught—even though we should be able to act on our own free will, anyway—is equally terrifying, and I shudder to think what would happen should the plan fail.

But, as scary as both scenarios are, I know a choice needs to be made. And time is running out to make it.

.

The night has come.

I am wide awake in the dark, sitting by my unlit fire-place, still unsure as to what to do. The anxiety makes my chest feel tight as I toil with a decision that I seem incapable of making. From my position seated in the chair, I can see out of the room's window, and the view is of the hill on the edge of town—the same hill that I will need to climb if I am to join my friends.

Movement outside catches my attention, and I see a figure creep towards the base of the incline, sticking to the undergrowth and shrubs as they move. Even in the dark, I recognise it as Maria. She stops just before where her ascent would begin and turns to face my house. I can't see her face clearly from this distance, or make out her expression—I have no idea if she can see me, but I can almost sense her judgmental gaze.

My cowardice has disappointed her.

I know that from our exchange earlier, and the shame I feel from it weighs heavily on me, yet I can still not bring myself to leave the relative safety of my house. Something inside me screams that following my friends out there will lead to my death, and that they are now walking on to theirs.

Or is that just my timid and cowardly nature talking? Which would, likely, paralyse me with such fear that I'll be stuck here in this village—under the rule of that vile Agnes Sibbett—for the rest of my days. Am I such a pathetic excuse for a woman that I would give up on what I know is right, just because of fear?

Maria makes her way up the hill to the crest. From somewhere within, I finally find some courage and decide that I must leave with them. Whatever dangers lie out there in the forest, it has to be safer than staying here, so I get to my feet and run out of the front door, out into the cool night air, and quickly make my way over to the base of the hill. I see Maria go over the crest and disappear from sight. I want to yell to get her attention so that she will wait for me, but know that in doing so, I will draw attention. So, I stay quiet.

And, no sooner do I reach the foot of the incline, than I hear it. Sudden and pained shrieks from above. One of which, I am certain, is from Maria. The horrible sounds chill me to my core, and I know instantly that people are dying up there.

Whatever bravery I found inside that brought me out here suddenly disappears in an instant, and I find myself running back inside to the safety of my front room—the cries of agony rolling in the night air, chasing me as I go like ghostly wails. Once inside, I kneel below my window and peek my head up just enough to see out. The sounds suddenly cease, but I now see someone at the top of the hill, looking down, like a ruler looking over their kingdom.

It is Sibbett. And she is covered in blood.

But it is not the sight of Agnes Sibbett that frightens me

so much that I physically gasp. It is the glimpse of the thing that stands behind her.

A daemon.

A terrifying thing. Simply gazing at it is enough to make my heart hammer in my chest and my joints lock in fright. I let myself fall to the floor, terrified that either of them might see me. And I quietly cry for the rest of the night, knowing that my friends are now dead, and that I am trapped in this hell.

One year later...

My life is a misery. I drift through my days like a ghost, always trying to be invisible, to keep my head down so as not to upset the wrong person for fear word will get back to Mother Sibbett.

That is how our leader is now known. It is not Agnes, anymore, and she has assigned herself as mother to all of us. The leader of our flock. And she spends most of her time within the church. A secretive place, that only a chosen few are allowed to enter.

Most who aren't in that inner circle are, in fact, trying their utmost to gain her favour and trust. But there are still those of us that do not like what is happening and keep our heads down for fear of death... or worse.

Stories have circulated of strange things happening during the midnight sermons in that church. Ghastly, inhuman things. Disgusting acts of depravity that no human should even think about, let alone take part in. Deeds of sodomy and sacrifice of man, woman, and beast alike.

These are only stories, of course, whispered between the

shunned, the unworthy, but it is difficult not to believe them. Because it is clear to see the change in those close to Mother Sibbett.

The changes come not only in the way they act, but in their physical appearance, too. Their features are... different. At first, I thought I was imagining things, but it has since become quite evident that what I am seeing is real, as I am not the only one to notice. But those that are changing—those who develop drooping eyes, cleft lips, twisted faces, and elongated limbs—do not seem to want to hide what is happening to them. It is almost a badge of pride, proof that Mother Sibbett has chosen them and deemed them worthy.

They believe they have been touched by the thing Mother Sibbett worships and obeys.

For you see, it is not God that is worshiped in that damned church. Oh no, it is something else entirely. Not once have I heard any of them refer to God, or Our Lord. However, I have heard mention of ancient things, unknown truths, and Old Ones. At first, I believed that the church was constructed to worship the Devil—Satan himself—but now I know that they believe in something different. Something *more*. And something infinitely more evil and insidious.

And I am worried.

More-so than usual, as I feel a sense of history repeating itself. People are whispering and conspiring again. It is just like it was with Maria and Robert... and look what happened to them.

Those that are shunned from Mother Sibbett and the inner circle—those that distrust her and what is going on here—have decided they want to know what is happening in the church. They want to know exactly what they are a part of simply by living in this village, and to know what is being kept from them.

I fear it will not end well. In fact, I *know* it won't. Maria, Robert, and my other friends went against Mother Sibbett, and they were killed. No one has confirmed this outright, but Sibbett and Henry and the others have never tried to quash rumours of the that group's demise, simply shrugging and saying 'I don't know,' but with a sneering look that instead says, *They died, alright, and you will too, if you don't fall in line*.

But I will have no part of any of it. I will keep my head down and try to keep existing here without being noticed. I will be a ghost.

I watch from my window again, just as I did the night Maria and Robert were killed. But it is a different window this time, with a different view. My eyes are now focused on the centre of the village, which I can see from the front of my house.

I can see the well and the church, even in the dead of night.

There is a sermon going on inside of the church, and I notice the flickering of candlelight through the building's high windows. And, because of the glow cast by this light, I can also see the huddled figures of those who want to know more approaching that place of worship. The curious off to investigate, as they promised they would.

I will be no part of it. Whatever they see or learn, I know, will do nothing to help any of us.

As they get close, about six of them, the doors to the church slowly open, and the moving villagefolk stop dead in their tracks. Mother Sibbett appears out of the darkness, wearing a simple black dress with a high collar and long, basic skirt which falls to the floor over her feet. She beckons the villagers inside. She says something, I can see her mouth move, but at this distance I cannot hear her speak. After a moment's hesitation, the curious ones seem to accept the invitation and enter the church. The door is closed behind them. And, for the longest while, all is quiet. The only sound I hear is a faint bleating from my goat Ollie, who is tethered just outside.

But then the noises start.

Hideous wails and agonising screams. I am yet again reminded of that fateful night a year ago when many of my friends died. I feel the same terror and absolute fright—so strong and sudden that it incapacitates me, freezing me to the spot, forcing me to look out of the window, even though I dearly don't want to.

I know other people in the village can hear what is going on, as well. Those, like me, who are now cowering and hiding in their houses. But no one comes out to see what is happening. I will not go out to help, either.

I want this madness to end. I want to pull myself away from the window, crawl beneath a blanket, and force my eyes shut. Whether I sleep or not, I will lie there all night until the coming day, and then fantasise, yet again, of making my escape from this place and the darkness that has consumed it and its inhabitants.

But when I see the main doors of the church open slightly again, and a terrified person slip out and sprint across the centre of the village—straight for my house—I know none of that will happen. I see that it is a man named William, someone I spoke to only yesterday. The closer he gets, the more detail I can make out: he is naked, covered in red and black smears, and his eyes are wide with absolute terror. No one follows him from the church, and the door has drifted shut behind him. I suspect that Sibbett and her congregation do not know he has escaped.

But why is he coming here to me? Panic rises, as I'm fearful I will somehow get drawn into his mess.

Go away, go away, go away.

He runs up to my door and kicks it open. 'Help me, Eileen,' he says, breathless.

'Quiet,' I bark.

He shuts the door and drops to the floor, sobbing. 'We have to hide. We have to leave.' Tears are streaming down his face, and his body won't stop shaking. 'It is madness, Eileen. It is a nightmare made flesh. Our souls are damned. We cannot stay.'

'Quiet!' I repeat myself. I walk over to him with a blanket and drape it over him. I like William, but by coming to me for help, he could have doomed me as well.

'The things they do in that church, Eileen. And the thing that they summon. It is Hell. Hell made real. And now we are trapped.'

I hear a commotion outside and run back to the window. People are pouring out of the church—all of Sibbett's chosen ones. All the twisted and changed minions. And now, for reasons I cannot explain, their change has only intensified. They almost don't look human anymore.

Mother Sibbett comes out last, and I notice that she is carrying something. I let out a gasp as I realise it is a human head: Henry's. His eyes have been gouged out, and his mouth gapes open as if in an eternal scream.

'Out of your homes!' comes the bellowing cry from Mother Sibbett as she stands in the centre of the village, surrounded by her army of misshapen followers.

Her voice is loud—louder than should be possible—and has a certain... otherworldly quality to it. Her appearance has changed as well, like her fellow congregation, and she is completely naked. On her filthy skin I can see small white orbs, like small sacks, each with a small dark dot that moves around.

Are those things eyes?

Fear is all that I have known for the past few years, but now the horror I am feeling hits new heights.

'Out! Now!' Sibbett commands.

'We can't,' William sobs to me from his seated position in the other room. 'We'll die.'

I see some people mill out from their homes, but not many. Sibbett shakes her head.

'Fetch them!'

And, at once, all of her minions move en-masse. They break into people's houses and pull them out, kicking and screaming. They come for me and I panic, grabbing a knife I keep close to my bed, terrified that I may actually have to use it.

My door is quickly broken down and I am pulled—along with William—out to the town centre as well. I am unable to put up a fight but manage to tuck the blade beneath my garments before it is noticed or taken from me.

I scream and plead for mercy but am completely ignored as I'm dragged close to the well, along with my fellow villagefolk. Those of us who are not with Mother Sibbett—those of us who are normal—are penned in by the rest, like sheep surrounded by hungry wolves. I feel someone stand close to me and take my hand. It is George, now almost a man and close to eighteen years of age, and I feel reassured by his presence. But I see equal fear in his eyes, as well.

Something is happening, that much is clear.

'My servants,' Mother Sibbett says to us all. 'My dear, sweet friends. I know many of you are desperate to know why you have not been taken in to my favour and feel cast aside. Well, tonight, that will all change. Tonight, you will all become my children. All you need to do is to accept my rule and renounce your false God.'

The only response from the people held prisoner was fearful sobbing. Someone, I don't know who, manages the courage to yell, 'Let us go.'

Mother Sibbett just laughs. 'My children, the God you all worship is a lie. He is not real. Just an imaginary story told to you by someone scared of dying. But there are things that do exist, that are infinitely more powerful than we are. It is one such ancient being that I serve—the one who claims dominion in this forest. We are in its home, here, and we belong to it. Pledge your lives and your souls to me, or face eternal damnation.'

No one says anything, because what can a person really say to that? It is terrifying madness.

After being greeted with silence, Mother Sibbett begins to laugh. A horrible cackle, completely devoid of humour, laced only with cruelty. She laughs so hard I see tears spill down her cheeks.

'Have it your way,' she says, shaking her head. 'For what it's worth, no matter the answer you gave, the result was always going to be the same. Your souls now belong to me. And I am here to collect.'

Excited murmurs rise up around those gathered with her—the hungry wolves who are keeping us trapped in the village centre.

Mother Sibbett throws Henry's head to the ground and then runs a bloody hand over her sagging breast. She licks her lips, and I see those horrible, alien eyes on her skin flit about excitedly.

'Time to indulge.'

And with that, her minions pounce.

7-11

It is chaos around me as my fellow villagers are taken prisoner.

But some of them are fighting back, and a melee has broken out. I see George throw his right hand and connect with an approaching servant of Mother Sibbett. I hear the crunch of bone and cartilage and see blood squirt from beneath the buried fist as the shocked man's nose crumples beneath it. The man takes two steps back at the impact and clutches his face, howling in pain.

And then I am pulled away, dragged through the fighting and wrestling as the followers of Mother Sibbett start to gain dominance, which is no surprise given their greater numbers. But George, who I have only really seen as a boy up until now, acts like he is possessed, and with a single purpose. He kicks out at someone else who approaches, and headbutts yet another. I feel a hand grasp me from behind, but George drags me powerfully away and, though my clothes tear, I slip free from the restrictive grasp of the unknown assailant.

Soon we break free of the crowd and rush out of the

village centre to the tree line that surrounds it. I notice some other villagers have broken through as well, and all are skittering out in different directions.

But all of us are pursued. Escape will not be easy.

And so it proves.

As we rush through into the trees—running for our very lives—I turn my head and see two men closing in. Their movements are not quite normal, almost animalistic as they bound through the trees, sometimes using hands to spring forward from the ground. And they are so fast as well. I know they will catch us, and that we will die. Me and poor young George, who has just started his life, and who is always a ray of sunshine despite losing his parents years ago.

He doesn't deserve this. But I know he will be caught.

Unless...

'George,' I say, panting, 'you need to keep going.'

'I am,' he said. 'Keep up.'

'No. Keep going without me.'

He turns to look at me as we continue to run, the air burning in my lungs. And the men giving chase continue to get closer and closer.

'I can't leave you behind.'

'You... must.' Speaking is hard, and I have to take quick breaths between words. 'I can't outrun them. You can.'

'But—'

'Promise me,' I say, cutting him off. 'You need to warn the other towns. Or we will have died for nothing.'

He makes as if to argue more, but I push him, forcing him forward, and then turn to face my pursuers. Casting a glance over my shoulder, I am relieved to see that George—even though he looks back to me with a look of sadness—has heeded my words and kept going. And now I know I have to show confidence and aggression and fight, for once in my miserable life. I need to keep these two monstrous men away from him.

I clench my teeth and ball my fists. Both men carry a look of evil and arrogance on their twisted faces. I pull out my knife and, when they are close enough, launch myself at them, screaming with all the rage and anger I can muster.

I don't know much of what happens, only that I flail my arms around and try to bury the blade into whomever I can. I soon feel it sink into flesh, and I hear one of them cry out. But, at the same time, I am bundled easily to the ground. Both try to restrain me, so I kick and fight with everything I have. I know this is a battle I will lose, but I just need to give George enough time.

As one man grips my arms, and another my legs, I manage to turn my head, to look and see how much distance George has put between us. I think I manage a smile as I am just in time to see him disappear beyond the trees.

Goodbye, George, my sweet boy.

Still I fight on, swearing at my demonic attackers, and making this as difficult as possible. My blade cuts and slashes, and then finds itself buried into meat once again. Another howl of pain. I don't know how long I fought against them, but I feel my strength quickly sapping, and I don't have much left in me.

Eventually, I see one of them lift a rock and bring it down on my head. There is a flash of white and blinding pain. Then... only darkness.

When I wake, my head feels like it is about to explode from the pain I feel. I do not want to be conscious, as this only brings agony that throbs and blooms from my temples.

It takes a moment for my memory to catch up to me and for my vision to focus. I remember the fight with the two men as I gave myself up in order for George to escape. I pray to God that I was successful.

I realise that I am being dragged. Looking up, I see through blurred vision that the two man who attacked me are now moving me, each holding an arm, pulling me along, face down. My legs and shins scrape across the dirt ground. I am back in the village, and I see many dead people being thrown into the well. And the things that have been done to these poor souls—their bodies mutilated and torn asunder. And it breaks my heart to see they are both men and woman, old and young.

I cry.

But, it seems, that well is not my fate. There are sounds coming from within the church. Screams of agony and wails of pleasure. And that, I realise, is our destination. I am dragged inside, through the large double doors that both lay open.

And I finally see the inside of this damned place. But I wish to God I hadn't.

I am brought before Mother Sibbett.

She stands—in all her naked grotesqueness—at the front of this church on a slightly elevated platform. I see Ollie, my goat, tethered up there with her, which confuses me. Sibbett's servants are everywhere, and many of the unfortunate villagers—those that have not been cast into the well—are present as well. They are all screaming for help as a sickening torture is beset upon them.

Sodomy.

Desecration.

Sexual acts and horrific violence. I see that some are even being stitched together while they are alive, fused into positions of vile acts against God. The pain those people must be in...

I fear that is to be my fate as well.

And I also see that others have been strewn about the interior of the church, tied to timber beams high above, or mounted on the walls. Some are dead, dismembered, and others still living, though gutted or mutilated. Those that are alive will no doubt die soon.

I am thrown to the ground at the filthy, claw-like feet of Mother Sibbett, and she sneers down at me. I can see those horrible eyes that line her body: milky white sacks of puss with small, jet-black pupils.

I do not know what she is turning into—what kind of transformation she is going through—but I do know that it is undoubtedly against God, and I will have no part of it.

I am going to die, of course. I know that now. But, as long as I resist, I believe my soul will be taken and protected by the warm embrace of my Lord.

'Little mouse,' Sibbett says in a mocking tone. 'Do you see the power of the God that I worship? Not a false deity, as all you pathetic sheep blindly follow, but something real. Something terrible. And it has shown me things, given me knowledge that has... changed me.' She smiles. Her teeth are cracked and blackened. 'And now, it is time for us to give ourselves to it completely. I will be released from this mortal coil and become something more. And...' Now she leans in close, so that only I can hear her. I can smell her rancid breath—like rotten cabbage—as it blows over my face. 'The rest of you will come with me, and belong to me forever.'

She stands up again and begins to laugh. I hear Ollie bleat. Sibbett takes a few steps back, and I see her retrieve an axe. My heart drops as she walks over to my pet. She raises the tool, and I admonish myself for being such a pathetic coward in life. I have stood by and done nothing as this vile hag has taken over our community. We all have. Perhaps we deserve what is coming because of that.

The axe falls, taking off poor Ollie's head. Sibbett cackles her pleasure.

Something in me snaps.

I am on my feet, rushing towards her, hands outstretched. It is a rage beyond anything I had felt when fighting off my attackers earlier. I just want to kill this vile wench, and I will give anything... absolutely anything... to make that happen. She can have my soul, for all I care, I just want to make her suffer. But she just smiles as I wrap my hands around her neck. I hear something behind her. A deep, inhuman growl, and then I see it, the same thing I saw behind her the night Maria and Robert died up on the hill.

The daemon. It is changed somewhat now, its form different, and the sight of it causes my heart to seize. It is simply too much to look at, and I feel like my eyes may slip from my skull and my mind implode from madness. I drop to my knees, clutching my chest, unable to give voice to the scream lodged there.

Sibbett again brings up the axe again and swings. There is pain. My vision spins as my head is removed.

I should be dead.

But I am not.

My body is defiled. I can still see, though how that is possible, I do not know. And the eyes through which I now view the world are not my own.

The head of my pet was sewn to my neck, turning us into one twisted effigy. My body is positioned in a way that seems to have meaning to Sibbett. Legs crossed, one arm held up. Sticks and rope and twine used to display me.

All I feel is unrelenting terror that never ends. From my position, I am able to witness what happens to my fellow villagers. The evil bestowed upon them. And then the fire starts, and Sibbett and her remaining congregation—as well as my own dead body—are engulfed and destroyed in violent flame.

And yet, still I am not dead. Well, that is not quite true. My mortal body is destroyed, but somehow I continue to exist in a state that makes no sense to me. I now belong to two worlds, pulled back and forth between them at will by Mother Sibbett and the thing that she follows. Sometimes I exist in my own world, always stuck in the same position, with Ollie's head in place of my own.

But when I'm not there, prostrated as Mother sees fit, I am somewhere else. Somewhere I do not understand. A nightmarish place where the pain and torture are infinite. I see creatures and maddening monsters that are beyond comprehension. And over the many hundreds of years, none of it becomes more bearable for me.

This is my existence. A puppet for Mother. And I now find myself back in my own world, in the forest of the damned, as four new poor souls enter, unknowing what is to come.

And I can do nothing to help them.

I know that at some point they will see me like this, shown to them by my master, as has happened countless times before. And I will see the look of horror as they gaze upon my vile appearance.

And then they will die, and their souls will join mine in eternal Hell.

Forever.

FOREST OF THE DAMNED

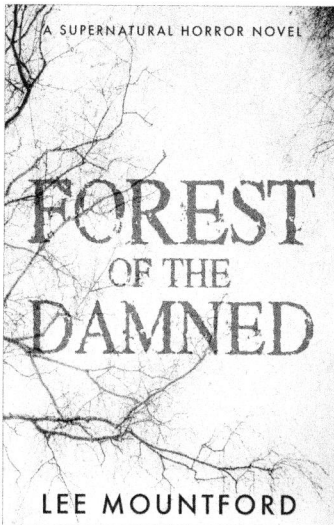

The Black Forest is a prequel to my fifth full-length novel, *Forest of the Damned*. That story follows the four hikers we see at the end of The Black Forest, as they unwittingly enter the domain of the evil Mother Sibbett.

Buy *Forest of the Damned* now.

HAUNTED: PERRON MANOR

A TERRIFYING HAUNTED HOUSE NOVEL.

Haunted: Perron Manor

Book 1 in the Haunted Series.

Sisters Sarah and Chloe inherit a house they could never have previously dreamed of owning. It seems too good to be true.

Shortly after they move in, however, the siblings start to notice strange things: horrible smells, sudden drops in temperature, as well as unexplainable sounds and feelings of being watched.

All of that is compounded when they find a study upstairs, filled with occult items and a strange book written in Latin.

Their experiences grow more frequent and more terrifying, building towards a heart-stopping climax where the sisters come face to face with the evil behind Perron Manor. Will they survive and save their very souls?

Buy Haunted: Perron Manor now.

FROM THE AUTHOR

I sincerely hope you enjoyed this collection of short horror stories. I've tried to make them as varied as possible, ranging from the creepy to the gory, and even to the melancholy and sad.

As with all my books, this was a labour of love. And, let's be honest, if you are diving into the deepest and darkest regions of your mind and talk about death and mutilation, then you've got to enjoy doing it. But I firmly believe that shining a light on such things is healthy. Far from making us weird and depraved psychotics, it actually lets us explore the darker side of human nature, and how we handle fear, only we get to do so with the safety blanket of reality wrapped around us. Indeed, I always tend to find that fans of horror are among the most well-adjusted people I know. Usually...

So, if these stories were to your tastes (and if they were, congratulations on being a weird and depraved psychotic!), then please consider checking out my full-length novels, which are all listed in the Bibliography section of this book.

Be warned, they are every bit as dark as the preceding stories, if not more so.

If you have enjoyed this book, then please consider leaving a review on Amazon.

Thank you for reading.

- Lee

JOIN THE FACEBOOK GROUP

Remember to join my Facebook Group if you haven't already. There, I am able to talk with my readers much easier than via email, and we have some great conversations. It is a lively, friendly place, and I try to give as much as possible there (such as example chapters for upcoming books, as well as running polls to help readers decide on covers, book names and more).

If that sounds like your kind of thing, just follow the link and join up! I can't wait to see you there:

Facebook Group - Click Here

BIBLIOGRAPHY

All of the novels listed below take place in the same shared universe. While The Demonic, The Mark, and Forest of the Damned, all lean more towards the creepy and building dread, and deal with haunting, ghosts and demons (and therefore form my Supernatural Horror Series)—my other books, Horror in the Woods and Tormented, are much more full on, edge-of-your-seat shockers full of blood and gore.

But all of these stories are dark, shocking, and—hopefully—scary as hell.

The Supernatural Horror Series:
   The Demonic:
   Danni thought she knew fear…
   But this house will show her what it is to be truly afraid.
   Called back to a childhood home, she must lay to rest a father that made her life hell. But something else waits for her in that house. Something far beyond what she could possibly imagine. Restless spirits and an insidious demon ensure this homecoming is one of nightmares.

Can Danni save her family... and her very soul? To do so, she must face the ghosts of her past as well as an ancient and malevolent evil.

The Mark:

It isn't the house that's haunted...

It's the person.

Kirsty is no stranger to trauma, but when her house is invaded one night, she is left with a strange mark carved into her skin.

And that is when the horrifying ghosts start to appear.

As the experiences grow more frequent—and dangerous—Kirsty must fight for her life and unravel the mystery behind the occult symbol etched into her flesh. This forces her into the terrifying world of the occult, where she learns of a Bible written by the Devil himself.

Can she save her very soul from damnation?

Forest of the Damned:

Legend says this forest is haunted...

A group of four researchers travel to the Black Forest to investigate the stories surrounding the area. They hope to gather evidence that the paranormal is real.

But getting what they want could cost them their souls.

The forest soon delivers on its promise, but their excitement is ruined when one of the group disappears in the night. Ghostly apparitions, disembodied voices, and demonic things lurking in the darkness turn the adventure of a lifetime into a living nightmare.

And behind it all, the infamous Mother Sibbett waits, aiming to show them the truth of life after death.

Other Novels:

Horror in the Woods:

First they found a desecrated body...

... then hell followed.

Four friends spend a weekend hiking in the woods, getting back to nature, never imagining they would end up being hunted.

But they soon stumble into the territory of the sick and twisted Webb family—psychopaths with a taste for human meat. And these monsters are hungry.

Will the group make it out of the woods alive? To do so, they will have to face these cannibals head-on, and unravel the secret behind the twisted family's very existence.

You will love this brutal, gory, and violent horror story, because it raises the tension on every page and will leave you exhausted and drained.

Tormented:

This isn't hell... it's far worse.

Insidious experiments are being carried out at Arlington Asylum, and the only way the inmates ever leave is inside a body bag.

Adrian is a prisoner here. And he is next on the list to receive the strange medicine that is being administered. Medicine that causes certain... changes... to those who take it.

If he is to survive, Adrian must find his self-worth and start fighting for his life while chaos erupts in the asylum around him.

Because these experiments open up a gateway to a place worse than hell. And the nightmarish inhabitants of that place break through and intend to tear our world apart.

Can Adrian stand against impossible odds and end this threat before it's too late?

The Netherwell Horror:

'Sis, I'm in trouble. Real trouble. And I need help.'

After receiving a worrying message from her estranged brother, Beth Davis sets out to find and help him, ending up in the strange, coastal town of Netherwell Bay.

There, she begins to witness terrifying and unexplainable things, and reports of ritualistic murders have the town panicked.

A sinister cult soon makes its presence known, and the dark history of Netherwell Bay is unveiled. Beth then finds herself in a race against time to stop a doorway to Hell from opening... permanently.

The Netherwell Horror is a Lovecraftian mystery that quickly descends into madness, sickening violence, and chaos. Fans of Silent Hill with love this nightmarish tale, but those of a squeamish disposition need not apply...

PRAISE FOR LEE MOUNTFORD

Praise for Lee Mountford

'It's been a long time since a novel actually scared me. The Demonic did just that.' - horrorafterdark.com (review of The Demonic)

'The Demonic, by author Lee Mountford, is a horror tour de force...It is scary. Truly scary.' - horrornovelreviews.com (review of The Demonic)

'Lee Mountford has already proved himself to be one of Britain's best horror writers working today, but The Forest of the Damned is his greatest achievement to date.' - Duncan Thompson, Horror Author (review of Forest of the Damned)

'All the while, Mountford keeps dropping these creepy, skin-crawling scenes on you and he does it with such a nice touch. There's a slow build-up of dread, as he builds the characters and atmosphere and slowly unwinds the story. At times, he dangles you over the edge for a few moments before he plunges you over

the edge. And this is where his storytelling is a cut above many of his peers.' - intothemacabre.com (review of The Mark)

'...the atmosphere was what really drew me into the novel. I loved the feel of the haunting, the visceral character reactions, and the damn clicking of that kid's crutches...' - Stuart Thaman, Horror and Fantasy Author (review of The Demonic)

'I think every fan of horror should read Horror in the Woods.' – Kendall Reviews (review of Horror in the Woods)

'Mountford nails the atmosphere in every single page of this novel.' - horroafterdark.com (review of Forest of the Damned)

'If you love talk of tearing flesh, chronicles of cannibalism, and descriptions of dismemberment, this book is for you.' – horrornovelreviews.com (review of Horror in the Woods)

'The terror felt real to me, and that is a reaction that takes a lot of talent to evoke in a reader... The Atmosphere created was incredibly tense, and fear practically poured off the pages.' - Horroafterdark.com (review of The Mark)

ABOUT THE AUTHOR

Lee Mountford was born and raised in the North East of England, in the small town of Ferryhill. Not much happens there anymore, but it has a surprisingly dark history... which probably helped cultivate his love of horror.

He is a best-selling author with a huge passion for the dark, the scary, and the macabre.

He still lives in the North East of England with his amazing wife, Michelle, and his two daughters, Ella and Sophie.

For more information
www.leemountford.com
leemountford01@googlemail.com

OTHER BOOKS BY LEE MOUNTFORD

The Supernatural Horror Collection
The Demonic
The Mark
Forest of the Damned

The Extreme Horror Collection
Horror in the Woods
Tormented
The Netherwell Horror

Haunted Series
Inside Perron Manor (Book 0)
Haunted: Perron Manor (Book 1)
Haunted: Devil's Door (Book 2)
Haunted: Purgatory (Book 3)
Haunted: Possession (Book 4)
Haunted: Mother Death (Book 5)
Haunted: Asylum (Book 6)
Haunted: Hotel (Book 7)
Haunted: Catacombs (Book 8)
Haunted: End of Days (Book 9)

Darkfall Series
Darkfall: Deathborn (Book 1)
Darkfall: Shadows of the Deep (Book 2)
Darkfall: Crimson Dawn (Book 3)

ACKNOWLEDGMENTS

Thanks first and foremost to my editor, Josiah Davis (http://www.jdbookservices.com), for such an amazing job.

The amazing cover was supplied by Debbie at The Cover Collection (http://www.thecovercollection.com).

Thanks as well to fellow author—and guru extraordinaire—Iain Rob Wright, for all of his fantastic advice and guidance. If you don't know who Iain is, remedy that now: http://www.iainrobwright.com. An amazing author with a brilliant body of work.

And the last thank you is the most important—to my amazing wife, Michelle, and my daughters, Ella and Sophie. You three are my world. Thank you for everything.

❀ Created with Vellum

Printed in Great Britain
by Amazon